One Elven

Inquisition

A Woke Fairy Story

STEVE WILEY

Ordering Information:

Quantity sales. Special discounts are available on
quantity purchases by bookstores, corporations,
associations, and others. For details, contact the
publisher at the email address above.

Orders by U.S. trade bookstores and wholesalers may
also order directly from Ingram Spark.

ISBN: 978-0-9981492-9-5

Warning

Content may be deemed offensive by
transracial ogres, marginalized mermaids,
polyracial pansexuals, archbishops of
gender studies, chief creature officers,
Spanish donkeys, trolls, social justice
warriors, Albert Einstein, and the
inquisition itself...

Death by Fire

Finbar Finnegan was quite literally *hoofing* it across town to work. You see, Finbar was a faun, complete with cloven hooves, the hairiest legs in the land, and horns like the devil. Not that he looked in any way devilish. He looked like Mr. Tumnus, minus the goatee. Finbar considered himself sufficiently goatish without the goatee.

Finbar was clip-clopping his way through the marketplace on his way to work when he noticed an elf bound to a large wooden stake, about to be burned alive. Although an elvish burning at the stake was hardly an uncommon occurrence, Finbar stopped a moment to watch. It was hard to walk by a stake-burning without at least stopping for a glance.

A crowd of spectators was gathering. There was *always* a crowd. The masses loved a good old fashioned public execution and/or torturing. Suffering was at the very core of nearly all drama and entertainment, and was treated as such in the kingdom. Higher-profile executions were often publicized by broadsheets and other official proclamations around town. The spectators picnicked and laughed, as if the gruesome ritual were no more than a free-of-charge, government-sponsored theatrical production.

Finbar watched as a jawless troll stepped forward, reading aloud the charges.

"Sir elf, you stand before this holiest of tribunals accused of heresy. Ministry evidence suggests that you have publicly made claims that there exists an innate, biological difference between mermaids and goblins. Furthermore, you have claimed mermaids are underrepresented in industries traditionally dominated by goblins, such as mining, not as a result of sexism and racism, but because of biological differences between mermaids and goblins. Specifically, you claim mermaids are underrepresented in the mining industry due to their preference for water, over the generally dryer conditions present within mines. Do you deny these accusations?"

"I do not." There was a squeaky tinge of fear in the elf's voice.

"Then you admit to harboring heretical gender and racial stereotypes?"

"I d-d-d—I do." The elf's teeth were chattering.

"Do you ask the tribunal for forgiveness?"

"Yes. I do. Please. Mercy! MERCY!"

The troll stepped back, joining a group of other trolls to discuss the fate of the elf. Meanwhile, the elf closed his eyes and began praying to himself. The crowd muttered with impatience. Finbar was also impatient. He had to get to work.

After only a few minutes, the troll tribunal came to the expected decision. The crowd fell silent as the same jawless troll spoke to the accused.

"Due to the severity of your crimes, forgiveness is denied. The concepts of 'goblin' and 'mermaid' are social constructs, intentionally established by your own elvish ruling classes to justify the segregation and subjugation of such groups. Furthermore, mermaids are equally capable of performing all those jobs goblins perform, including mining."

The troll paused for dramatic effect.

"This tribunal sentences you to death by fire. Any last words?"

"Mermaids don't work in mining because they're GODDAMNED MERMAIDS!" The elf was sobbing, screaming hysterically, shaking as if he were mad. "Mermaids and goblins *are* different! What's wrong with that? WHAT?"

The elf continued pleading as two trolls approached with torches and ignited the pile of wood beneath him. The fire spread quickly in the morning breeze. Plumes of smoke floated over the marketplace. The crowd stared, silent with expectation. Finbar stayed only until the flames reached the elf's toes. He never watched anything more than the toes catch fire.

Burnt toes were all he could stomach. Besides, he had to get to work. He was running late.

Finbar's office was only a few blocks away from the marketplace. He galloped down the sidewalk as fast as he could. Just before he walked through his office door, he was stopped in his tracks by the piercing death bellow of the engulfed elf. It was deafening, seeming loud enough to puncture an eardrum. Finbar fled from the awful howl into work, accidentally smashing one of his horns on the door frame, chipping off some paint.

"Damn it! I need a coffee," he groaned to himself.

-

Finbar loved coffee. Drank it night and day. He liked it black, with a hint of sweet cream, which turned it a cabernet color. Finbar liked his coffee like his wine – red. Fauns worship red wine, and every other color wine. Some said they invented it, way back in the Cult of Dionysus days. After which they invented the orgy, or maybe that invented itself. Hard to say for certain. One fact which is absolutely certain is that fauns love a finely fermented glass of grapes.

Finbar had plenty of other interests. He was an avid reader, able to navigate the local library blindfolded. He was a lover of the literary arts and much else that was artistic, passing many a weekend at the kingdom art museum. He went to the theatre, on the rare occasion he had money to go to the theatre. He didn't have much money because he didn't need much money. He was a minimalist. He lived in a modest apartment. He wore simple clothing. He listened to minstrel music. He meditated. Well, he tried to meditate. Fauns couldn't sit still. Too busy-brained to sit still. Blame that on the coffee. Or the wine.

Finbar was a cultured faun, from the cultured kingdom of Fantasmagoria, which lay beyond the known world, but was not so cunningly hidden as other uncharted realms like Wonderland or Neverland. It was located somewhere much more accessible to the average fantastical being and occasional human. No need to chase a rabbit down a hole, or pass the second star to the right and go straight on 'til morning. Any old boat could get you to Fantasmagoria. Being less exotic than those other fantasy lands, it was much more civilized. Maybe too civilized. The government liked it that way.

The Ministry of Equality was the ruling branch of government in Fantasmagoria. It was also the only branch of government. All governmental power and responsibility was concentrated in the Ministry of Equality. The Ministry did everything. It promoted the rule of law, supported the economic system, provided public services, defended the kingdom, and, of course, ensured equality among citizens. Equality was far and away the most important government function. The Ministry was obsessed with equality. So obsessed, they started an inquisition for the purpose of eradicating inequality.

Its formal name was the Holy Inquisition of Equitability. The mission of the inquisition was to combat all forms of inequality in the kingdom, by whatever means necessary. Any citizen or institution found to be contributing to the inequality of wealth, race or gender discrimination, economic immobility, or anything deemed remotely oppressive was swiftly and severely dealt with. Racism, sexism, heterosexism, ageism, ableism, classism, masculinism, and an endless list of other isms were punishable by death. Free enterprise was criminal. Individualistic tendencies were immoral. Conservative ideas were sinful. The mere belief that citizens were born different from the neck up could get your own neck chopped.

Elves were a frequent target of the inquisition for a variety of reasons. First and foremost, elves were viewed as economically advantaged. In an inquisition striving for absolute equality, being economically advantaged was a major disadvantage. Additionally, elves had a long, sordid history of intolerance and racism. Not that there was any evidence modern elves were racist and intolerant. The inquisition simply refused to let go of the past. It wasn't uncommon for charges to be brought forth for crimes committed generations before, by distant relatives.

Elves were not the only target of the inquisition. There was no class, race, or category of citizens fully immune from prosecution. Goblins, fairies, dwarves, druids, giants, even trolls had been tried and found guilty. Finbar once watched a djinn broken at the wheel for granting capitalistic wishes. First and last djinn he ever saw.

The inquisition was implemented by various tribunals scattered throughout the kingdom. Tribunals were courts of social justice made up of a dozen or so trolls and the odd ogre or stone giant, who was often needed for the apprehension and detainment of suspected heretics. The tribunals were responsible for virtually all inquisition-related activities within their jurisdiction. They investigated crimes, arrested heretics, conducted trials, passed judgment, and administered punishment. The Kafkaesque tribunals were feared by all, including Finbar.

There was rarely a fair trial for the accused. You were guilty until proven innocent. Troll tribunals were merciless. The public executions were constant, and often ghastly. There was no such thing as forgiveness, only retribution. Crowds prefer retribution. They swelled and rioted, mad with morality, as only the most devoutly religious can be. The mass hysteria created a culture of shame, anger, confusion, and despair. Instead of unifying the citizens of

Fantasmagoria, the Ministry of Equality and its inquisition divided them.

-

Finbar wasn't all that interested in politics.

It wasn't that he didn't believe in the stated mission of the Ministry of Equality. He wanted to help those less fortunate. He believed all citizens should be treated respectfully and given the same opportunities. He was sensitive to the kingdom's imperfect past and sympathetic to its victims. Finbar was a well-intentioned faun, but he questioned the intentions of the inquisition. Politics in Fantasmagoria were divisive, due in large part to the government's forced-belief systems and the incessant, bloodthirsty quest for a perfectly harmonious society.

There was no avoiding the inquisition, especially not for Finbar. Finbar worked as an editorial assistant for the *Elven Standard*, the longest running and most reputable newspaper in Fantasmagoria. As an editorial assistant, Finbar did very little actual editing. He performed more administrative work than anything, spending most of his days filing, scheduling, corresponding, and taking phone calls. It wasn't the most glamorous job on earth, but not bad for a faun with little experience who hoped to one day be a journalist himself.

At the newspaper, Finbar was suffocated with breaking inquisition stories. "If it bleeds, it leads," the editors preached. Finbar was always among the first to hear of tribunal investigations, high-profile trials, and grisly executions. The reign of terror was all the media reported, not because it was worth reporting, but because it sold newspapers. Fear and despondency were great for business. As it turned out, readers found bad news more interesting than good news.

Luckily for the newspaper, the bad news was never-ending.

The Not-So-Free

Press

Finbar had just sat down at his desk, cabernet colored coffee in hand, when the editor-in-chief stopped by for a surprise visit.

"Well, if it isn't Finbar the fandanglin' FINNEGAN!"

Finbar spat a mouthful of fresh coffee out in fandangled surprise. The editor-in-chief was a boisterous, rosy cheeked dwarf named Ivan, who was at least three hundred years old and had been in the newspaper business for most of that time. He was as friendly as he was loud and well-liked by all in the office, including Finbar.

"Good morning, Ivan. Need help with something?" Finbar asked as he wiped the coffee stains from his shirt.

"Sure as hell do! Got a new assignment for ya. It's quite important. The Ministry of Equality issued this new decree. Let me just say, it's gonna be a real pain in our asses, and I mean every inch of our asses from the peaks of our cheeks straight through the sphincter."

Finbar wasn't surprised at the news. The Ministry of Equality oversaw all companies, especially those in the media business. Journalistic guidelines were endless. Troll tribunals often visited the newspaper offices to inspect operations and ensure compliance with this or that. Major headlines were always first reviewed by a governmental redaction department.

"We got a delivery in the mail this morning from the government. It was a barrel-assed package labeled *Sensitivity Canon*. Inside was a list of words that have been made illegal." Ivan handed a thick manila envelope to Finbar. "Here's a list of the words and an explanation for the illegality. First, I need you to inventory and track all these wicked words. After you've done that, I need you to scan all of our upcoming articles for the words, censoring or replacing where necessary."

Finbar nodded to Ivan as he glanced down at the list of criminal words.

Salary: Classist, exclusionary term that may be deemed hurtful to unemployed and hourly-based workers.

Mumbo Jumbo: This phrase is derived from the elvish deity Maamajomboo. The Maamajomboo godhead was used by red elves to frighten and subjugate green elves into obedience for thousands of years.

Kiss: Trigger-inducing for the asexual community. Kiss-associated words such as naked, hump, and thrust should also be minimized.

Hooligan: This phrase is derived from the O'Houlihan clan of leprechaun immigrants who were starved and brutalized by their racist elvish overlords for dancing jigs and hoarding pots of gold at the end of rainbows. Terms like paddy wagon, bog trotter, and drunkard should also be avoided.

Balls: As in "Grow some goddamned balls, Bill." Inherently sexist, implies an individual needs a scrotum and testicles to gain courage and/or confidence.

No Can Do: This commonly used phrase was used to mock orcish immigrants who spoke broken English as they attempted to communicate when first arriving in Fantasmagoria.

World: Offensive to astral-gendered citizens, or those with a non-binary gender identity feeling deep connections and attractions to celestial bodies. Galaxy, cosmos, and space are adequate substitutes for world.

Finbar looked up at Ivan. "Kiss and balls will be tricky."

Ivan nodded his head in agreement. "Do this. Balls you just replace with nuts, until someone tells us not to. With kiss, I don't know what the hell to do. We've got a whole modern romance column we'll need to reassess. Try plugging smooch and peck where you can, and come to me with situations you're unsure of. Sound good?"

"Sounds good Ivan."

"Great. Thanks, Finbar. One other thing. The government is saying we'll start to get a list of words more often, maybe as often as every week. Are you good taking point with this, reading and censoring all these words going forward?"

"Happy to."

Truth was, Finbar was more than happy to. The censorship work beat the administrative humdrum of his usual day. And he believed in the spirit of the new decree. He had always considered himself careful in his choice of words. He believed sensitivity was important to a harmonious Fantasmagoria. If censorship could help the cause, why not?

Ivan slapped Finbar on the back, leaving him to sift through the formidable stack of banned words. It took Finbar most of the morning to rekey the words into the newspaper's vast database of rules and regulations. After he was done with that, he retrieved a draft of the following day's newspaper. Time to censor!

Finbar opened the newspaper, gasping at the utter lawlessness of the headline.

The Hooligan Kiss Heard 'Round the World

-

Finbar walked home from work that day. It was a fine day for walking. Summer was at its end. A wind came from the west, laden with the first autumn leaves of the season. The sun warmed Finbar from the cloudless sky above, the breeze blew him along from the work left behind, and the birds chirped from all around. There wasn't a troll in sight. Finbar breathed the remnants of summer air in deep, feeling calm and glad as he strolled down the sidewalk.

Finbar lived on the top floor of a three-story apartment on the corner of a quiet residential block lined with single-story brick bungalows. All the homes were occupied by families, except for this particularly beautiful blonde bungalow, where there lived an old, mysterious bachelor. Finbar admired the house whenever he passed by, but he only ever saw the old man on the windiest of days. It was the strangest thing; every single time the winds rose, the old man appeared on his front porch to greet them, like clockwork. Windy days were the only days he ever seemed to come outside.

As it was a blustery day, Finbar saw the old man as he walked down the block. Every single window of the house was opened, the curtains blowing every which way. The old man sat there with his eyes closed on the front porch swing, which faced the prevailing winds. The winds rocked the swing gently as he sat there, smiling the afternoon away. He looked as though there was nowhere in the world he'd rather be.

The old man opened his eye a sliver as Finbar passed by, giving him a friendly nod. Finbar nodded back, curious as to what spell the winds cast on the man.

When Finbar got home, he opened all his windows, inviting the wind in. He thought something might come of it, but nothing did. Finbar promised himself that someday soon he would ask the old man about the wind. He had a feeling there was a story worth hearing.

There was.

The Tipsy

Timepiece Tavern

Come nightfall, Finbar could normally be found with a snifter of spirits at the Tipsy Timepiece Tavern, his local watering hole. The tavern was snuggled between two ordinary homes on a residential street just a few blocks from Finbar's apartment. A quaint, two-story red brick cottage, it could have easily been mistaken for an ordinary house, were it not for the plaque above the door swinging gently in the wind, which read "Holy Grail Ale." Strings of ivy reached up each side of the brick near the front door like emerald sideburns. When the curtain of night closed over the neighborhood, the tavern's candlelit windows shone like cheerful beacons. Passing by, you could always see the smoking, drinking, and dancing silhouettes within.

Fantasmagoria had no shortage of bars, but the most genuine and friendly tended to be off the beaten path, away from the busy downtown, cleverly tucked away on quiet little streets. The Tipsy Timepiece Tavern was one of these. It was always filled with trusted regulars, which gave all who went there a sense of comradery and community. The place was a pleasant sanctuary from the stresses of everyday life and the horrors of the inquisition.

For many, including Finbar, the tavern was a home away from home.

-

The inside of the tavern was dimly lit that night, mostly from the candlewax-drenched chandelier overhead and smaller oil lamps on each of the tables. The stone fireplace crackled and popped, burning logs into woodsy smoke. The place was comfortably full of folks. There were dark elves, light elves, goblins, hobgoblins, mountain dwarves, hill dwarves, drunk dwarves, girls, guys, and golems. The reclusive neighborhood vampire even showed his face. You never knew if he was drinking red wine or blood, and no one dared ask, because there was absolutely no judging in a respectable tavern.

Finbar drank at the snug bar, which glowed faintly from the firelight dancing in the mirror behind it. He was joined by his bartender, who was also the owner of the tavern—*the* tipsy timepiece himself. You see, the owner of the tavern was a walking, talking grandfather clock. He was tall and thin, with stringy arms and legs, tangled silver locks, and a clock for a face. His timeless eyes shone between the hours of two and ten. He smiled from eight to four and wide as anything. His nose pointed out of the center dial. His name was Aristotle. He claimed to be related to that famous philosopher of the same name, and if you talked to him, you'd believe it. He was the sought-after sage of spirits. Locals came to Aristotle for advice about everything from affordable airships to mending relationships. Finbar came mostly for wine and conversation.

"Helluva day, Aristotle. *Helluva* day. *Elven Standard* got me censoring."

"Censoring *what* exactly?" Aristotle asked, sounding ruffled.

"Bunch of mumbo jumbo. Mostly insensitive stuff. Newly illegal language. The decree came straight my way from the Ministry of Equality, believe it or not. I'm moving up the corporate ladder fast, Aristotle. Yesterday, editorial assistant. Today, censor. Tomorrow, media tycoon!"

"So much for the free press," Aristotle grumbled. "The Ministry of Mindlessness calls all this inquisition business a 'cultural revolution' for social justice, equal rights, progress, blah, blah, blah. You know who else had a cultural revolution? Joseph Vissarionovich Stalin. How'd that go? Wonder how many censors he had on the payroll. You just be careful Finbar. First, it's linguistic censorship, then ideological censorship, the next thing you know you're assembling car seat covers fourteen hours a day in a Siberian reeducation camp."

"Is that so?" Finbar genuinely wondered if it were so.

"Sure as hell is, and speaking of hell, the road to it is paved with well-intentioned fauns. And don't you forget it..."

Finbar remembered to remember the road to hell as he sipped from his glass and looked out the window. It was a shivering, rainy night, the perfect sort to be sheltered from within a cozy tavern. Finbar watched the large raindrops, visible only within the orange orbits of lantern light outside or when they came splattering with great force upon the window. The occasional local splashed hurriedly by, hunched under an umbrella on the way home or to a local tavern. Finbar was about to order another round and engage the bartender in a philosophical debate on the moral necessity for suppression of speech when something unexpected appeared outside.

A unicorn.

The unicorn ambled by with its face turned to the ground, its drenched mane looking dreary as the weather. The poor creature was so covered in mud,

Finbar almost mistook it for a spotted horse. Unicorns weren't an uncommon sight in Fantasmagoria, but this one was different, because it was hornless. At first, Finbar hadn't noticed the disfiguration. The horn had been cut down to almost nothing. A bloody knob was all that was left. Another filthy, knobby-horned unicorn followed. Then another, and another. Finbar couldn't believe his eyes. Dozens of mutilated unicorns paraded sadly down the street.

"Jesus Harold Christ! Aristotle, there's half a herd of hornless unicorns walking by. Look!"

"Oh that." Aristotle looked out the window, unsurprised. "You didn't hear? A mob of trolls went stark raving mad in the marketplace today. They declared unicorn horns a menace. The trolls claimed the horns gave unicorns opportunities and advantages your average horse doesn't have. Unicorn privilege, as it were. The crowd got into one of those equitability frenzies. They just started lopping off unicorn horns left and right. Saddest sight you ever saw, and the sound was terrifying. You ever hear a unicorn horn crack?"

"No."

"Sounds like the chorus of all the saddest songs in the whole wide world, sung in an instant."

"Unbelievable. And to think, unicorns of all creatures. A unicorn never hurt a soul. What, what..." Finbar was at a loss for words. "What madness!"

"What madness?" Aristotle's eyes widened, and he leaned close to Finbar from behind the bar. "Why, the madness of crowds, of course. Creatures behave wonderfully well when you have them alone. But, that same seemingly civilized creature, when joined with an uncivilized crowd, is easily swayed by its madness and has a habit of becoming just as unruly. That's what happened today. Simple case of mad crowd disease. That's all an inquisition is, really. An epidemic of collective madness."

Others crowded around the bar windows to watch the disfigured unicorns walk by. Some of the barflies were horrified, spitting out their drinks in disgust. Others left for home, but most just stared. Finbar couldn't stand the sight. He turned away from the window and made his way to the jukebox, hoping for a little music to lighten the mood. The jukebox was a tall, wide cabinet of a music machine, complete with shiny hardwood veneers and glowing rainbow-colored bubble tubes percolating around the top. It had a latticed grille depicting what looked like the god Pan playing his pipes over the main middle speaker. The jukebox looked like it played magic, and it did. Most do.

Finbar dropped some change in and selected one of his all-time favorite songs. As soon as he heard the first chords, he put his glass down and started dancing by himself in the middle of the bar. He closed his eyes and sang the lyrics as he danced round and round.

Take your baby by the hair
And pull her close and there, there, there
And take your baby by the ears
And play upon her darkest fears
We were so in vies
In our dance hall days
We were cool on cries
When all you and everyone we knew

Could believe, do, and share in what was true.

Try playing that song, or anything from Wang Chung for that matter, and not falling under a dizzying, dancing trance. It's impossible not to, which explains why the rest of the tavern soon felt the musical magic and joined in. The dwarves joined hands in a circle around Finbar, tapping their boots together in a sort of space-aged square dance. Two gorgons danced wildly together on top of the bar. A goblin played air guitar. An overserved elf gyrated so crazily he spilled the pitcher of beer he carried. An elderly druid shook a leg. Even the doddering grandfather clock behind the bar was bobbing his head to the mystical beat. The whole tavern whirled and twirled, and in their revelry forgot about the storm outside, the mangled unicorns, and the inquisition.

Like I said—magic.

Church

One morning, Finbar polished his horns gold, shoed his hooves silver, put on his Sunday best, and went galloping to church. For the record, he didn't like church. In fact, he hated most everything about it: played out music, inane prayers, when to kneel, when not to kneel, sickly parishioners coughing, masses of elderly farting, newborn babies crying, and on and on. Still, he had to go. In the middle of an inquisition, it was wise to occasionally show your face in church.

Finbar walked to church that morning through a sea of freshly fallen leaves. Stray beer cans peeked out of the leaf-sea here and there like miniature tin boats.

The leaves were from the trees. The empty beer cans were from the students. Church was located on a college campus. In Fantasmagoria, all churches were required by law to be on college campuses. Universities played the dual role of educational and religious institutions, though they were far more religious than educational. Ideas were not freely exchanged. They were restricted. Dogmas were forced upon students and parishioners by professors, who were revered spiritual advisors. Mass was generally held within liberal arts and social sciences lecture halls.

Church was packed that morning. Finbar arrived early, but still too late to get a seat. He stood in the back, his view of the pulpit partially blocked by a massive stone slab on which was carved a list of the seven deadly "isms." Finbar read them over and over, reacquainting himself with them should anyone question his knowledge of the faith:

The Seven Deadly Isms

I. Individualism

II. Stoicism

III. Capitalism

IV. Conservativism

V. Commercialism

VI. Masculinism

VII. Geneticism

A glacial chill ran through Finbar's bones when he realized he had no earthly idea what stoicism meant. He might have been guilty of stoicism that very second without knowing it! He looked around nervously, making a paranoid mental note to research stoicism as soon as possible.

The church quieted and everyone stood at attention as the priest shuffled slowly down the center aisle. Finbar didn't recognize the priest, but he guessed he was some ancient race of forest troll. He was hunchbacked, with a weather-beaten, lichen-covered face under a thick red beard and long hair of amber leaves. Out of his head sprouted two giant antlers. He had to be helped up to the altar.

"Good morning to you all. My name is Mormulak, Archbishop of Gender Studies. I am delighted to be here. I was invited to the parish today to talk about victimhood, and the importance of weaponizing victimhood within marginalized communities to intimidate and topple elitist power structures. You may be seated."

Finbar sat down and listened, or tried to listen. He struggled to follow the old professor-priest. His attention span at church was a fraction of what it was everywhere else, and it wasn't particularly high everywhere else. The situation wasn't helped by the slowness and softness of the archbishop's voice. He sounded like a stoned Yoda.

"Must, must, must… Social status *must* only be gained through one's degree of victimization. The worst victims of historical oppression and atrocity *must* be anointed our future kings and queens. The moral high ground *must* in every case be held by those who are disadvantaged. We *must* actively promote an environment of never-ending outrage in response to historical injustices. Divergences from approved church opinion in these matters *must* be met with swift consequences."

Finbar's eyes blinked tiredly. He *must* stay awake. He pinched himself to get the blood flowing. Then stomped his hooves on the floor. Then plucked his hind leg hairs. He couldn't afford to close his eyes, not for a second. Staying awake in church was a matter of life or death.

"The devoutly pious must perceive everything in society as prejudiced, and presume negative attitudes in all those around us. History has taught us that even our most beloved figures, even those who claimed to be and seemed honorable, were not so. Peter Pan was an ageist rapscallion. King Arthur was a toxically masculine tyrant, reigning over a patriarchal Camelot. Harry Potter was a privileged, cisgender warlock. Hogwarts was an elitist, inherently discriminatory institution. Odysseus was an indiscriminate maniacal murderer. Albert Einstein was xenophobic. Miles Davis was a wife-beating misogynist. Helen Keller was a eugenicist. Alexander Graham Bell was eugenicist who feared deaf people. The good that is done in this life can *never* outweigh the bad. We must never forgive, or forget. Praise the Ministry."

"Ministry hear our prayers," the parishioners responded.

Finbar let roar a preposterous yawn. Half the church turned around at the sound. Finbar turned around himself, pretending to be clueless, as if it was the wall behind him that had yawned. Luckily for him, the old troll hadn't heard it and continued his sermon.

"The division of society into race-based groups that are either privileged, or not privileged, has of course helped to unify society. The only way to build a harmonious, multi-racial community is to amplify aggrieved differences between races within that community. The concepts of class and race-based guilt have aided government efforts in these areas. Elves are, of course, the most ungodly of all. To be born an elf is to be born with the stain of sin. Today's elves must be held responsible for the crimes of all past elvish cultures. Elvish guilt will effectively redress their many centuries of misdeeds. Amen."

"Amen," the parishioners responded.

Finbar closed his eyes, lost in a daydream. He dreamed of a world where he didn't have to go to church. Where everyone gave even less of a shit than him about religion, politics, grievances, oppression hierarchies, and original elvish sin. It was a world without the inquisition, where he could sleep in peace. A world where sleep was expected, even rewarded in church. He would be worshipped as the sleepiest sleeper. Sleep. Sleeeeeeeep...

Finbar fell asleep standing.

"Equity be with you," the Archbishop croaked.

"And also with you," the congregation responded, startling Finbar awake. His horns swiveled in a panic. He had no idea how long he was asleep for, but it seemed no one had noticed, thank heavens.

"Equity be with you" meant it was time for the dreaded sign of peace, which involved shaking hands with as many complete strangers in your general vicinity as possible. Finbar was a bit of a germophobe, so the practice naturally horrified him.

The shaking of hands started. Finbar looked

straight down, hands behind his back, trying to look most unfriendly. Using the no eye contact, surly strategy, he was limited to just three expeditious handshakes. Not bad. He was in the home stretch. A few parting words from the priest, and he would be a free man.

"As you go about your day, be hyper-vigilant to offense. Be ideologically pure. But more than anything, be wary. Most blasphemers, bigots, and racists don't realize they are these things. Unconscious transgressions are more rampant than ever. It is our duty as citizens to uncloak the masses of heretics. May the Holy Inquisition of Equitability bring justice to them..."

Finbar was gone before the prayer ended. That's the best part of sitting in the back of somewhere you'd rather not be. You're always the first to leave.

The Spanish Donkey

"What's a Spanish donkey?" Finbar asked a water sprite at the water cooler. The water sprite was on her way to a public torturing by Spanish donkey. Finbar was wondering whether to join her.

"It's a wooden donkey, dotted in razor-sharp spikes. The 'saddle' is an upside-down steel triangle, like a blunt butcher's saw. The condemned is stripped naked and tied onto the saddle so that their feet don't touch the ground. The torturers then tie weights to the ankles, so that the legs and genitals are smashed against the saddle and spikes. Once in a blue moon, the torturers splash the donkey-rider's feet with boiling water to really get them moving, and maimed."

"Sounds unnerving."

"It is. And not to be missed. You should absolutely come, if only for a little."

Finbar made the regrettable decision to stop by the spectacle on his way home from work that day. It was held in a vast meadow on the edge of town. Finbar arrived early, surprised to find the place already dense with spectators. He stood upon a crowded, hilly rise on the outskirts, peeking down around some trees and over heads toward the center of the meadow, where he saw the Spanish donkey. It looked like an over-sized, headless rocking horse, with little spikes like silver spots glinting in the sun all over the body. Finbar felt queasy just looking at it.

A band of trolls emerged from the shadows of a nearby glade with a distinguished-looking valley elf in tow. The elf was dressed in a dark three-piece suit, his face equally dark from the dried blood and mud covering it. He wore a crown of thorns to replace the crown of wildflowers normally worn by valley elves. One of his eyes was swollen shut, the other opened wide as could be. He winced as he walked, showing off a mouth of punched out teeth. He looked to have been freshly beaten, his body swaying with exhaustion as the trolls pushed him forward.

Soon, the center of the meadow was bustling with trolls. The accused was brought before a sadomasochistic troll who stood behind a podium upon a rickety wooden platform. The elf stood surprisingly straight as he faced the chief inquisitor. A few heads of cabbage pelted him as the charges were read aloud.

"You, sir, stand before this divine court accused of free enterprise, excellence, and excessive commercialism. Tribunal evidence indicates that in the past twelve months, your earnings have exceeded the governmental wealth ceiling established for those of elven ancestry. May I remind you, and all those in attendance today, that very ceiling was put in place to close the wealth gap in Fantasmagoria. Furthermore, our evidence indicates you have publicly made claims that the unequal distribution of assets among citizens exists not because of structural racism and gender discrimination, but as a result of inherent *genetic* group differences!"

The crowd gasped. Use of the word "genetic" alone was a serious crime.

"Furthermore, you have made claims that career success and wealth are strongly correlated with IQ. You have made claims that IQ is largely a result genetic heritability, and therefore will *always* vary collectively by race. Meaning, of course, that valley elves earn more money on average than the rest of Fantasmagoria because they are simply smarter. Is that a fair representation of your position? You believe valley elves are innately more intelligent than dwarves and fairies? You believe they are more intelligent than *trolls*?"

The bloodied elf raised his head defiantly.

"We're certainly more intelligent than *trolls*."

Finbar contained a laugh, along with the rest of the crowd.

"So then, you confess to exceeding the elvish earnings ceiling? You confess to denying that the Fantasmagorian wealth gap exists due to the endurance of an unfair socioeconomic order built on elvish dominance and power structures?"

"I confess to the truth."

"Do tell us of the truth."

"Intelligence has time and time again been shown to be a heritable trait, no different than height. The differences in group intelligence among elves, goblins, and dwarves can at least partially be explained by genetic factors. I'm sure environmental factors do play a role as well, but—"

"But what?" the troll cackled. "How convenient it is to be born a valley elf! It seems you have no control over your excessive wealth. You have no control over your contribution to inequality and the widening of the wealth gap in Fantasmagoria. *It seems you were just born that way!*"

The crowd cheered in approval. Chants of "Donkey! Donkey!" sprung up.

"This tribunal finds you guilty as charged," the

troll bellowed. "Tell me, sir elf. Do you like riding donkeys? I hear valley elves have a genetic predisposition for riding donkeys, especially the Spanish ones!"

The crowd went mad. They had come for blood, and were about to get it.

A gang of trolls swarmed the elf, first stripping off his clothes, then beating him unconscious. He regained consciousness the moment the trolls placed him in the saddle of the dreaded Spanish donkey. The elf's scream was unlike anything Finbar had ever heard. It was like a sonic boom, momentarily disorienting the whole crowd. For a few strange seconds, the meadow was silent and still, as if all were under some debilitating spell. All Finbar could hear was the wind whooshing through the branches above, rustling the leaves on the tips of the trees. A handful of leaves blew slowly through the air above the revolting scene. Finbar wanted to be blown away with them, but he couldn't. He found himself unable to move, or look away.

The trolls tied the elf's hands to head of the donkey

and each of his legs to a pole sticking up from the base. The condemned wiggled and wailed, seeming to pass in and out of consciousness, trying hopelessly to fall off the horse, which of course was impossible. The more he moved, the more he bled, in perfect agreement with the design of the monstrous device.

The elf screamed until his voice gave out, which didn't take long. All he could do then was sob hysterically. As he did, the trolls tied weights onto each of his ankles, which forced the elf down more firmly onto the jagged saddle of the donkey, further impaling his groin and inner thighs.

Shortly after the weights were secured, something snapped inside the elf. He started *riding* the donkey, bucking up and down in the saddle, laughing madly. He was bouncing up and down to hurry his own demise. He was bucking with such power, his whole body rose from the donkey, slamming back down into the steel teeth of the saddle with a gushing forth of blood that was so sickening the closest spectators turned away. The elf bucked and bucked until finally, after one especially high leap from the saddle, he came down to the echo of an eerie crack—the elf's sacral bone breaking. He stopped moving after that.

The crowd stared in quiet disbelief as the trolls untied the broken, still-bleeding elf from the donkey. Covered thoroughly in his own guts, the elf was unrecognizable. He could have been anyone, or anything. He could have been a troll, goblin, even a faun.

The chief inquisitor returned to the podium to address the crowd, a vile smirk on his face.

"Excellence leads to inequality…"

Stoicism and Reparations

Finbar sat at work one quiet morning reacquainting himself with the seven deadly isms, spending most of his time on stoicism. At church, it had dawned on him that he had no idea what stoicism was. It was important that he learn it, and how to avoid it. The penalty for stoicism was ordeal by water, or the tying of one's hands and feet together before being tossed into a lake. If the accused floated they were guilty. If they drowned they were innocent.

Finbar was busy reading stoic philosophy when he was interrupted by Miss Fox, the creature resources manager. Miss Fox was a shrewd and secretive red fox, rarely seen about the office. Normally, Finbar would have been nervous at being approached by the creature resources department, but not that morning. Miss Fox's tail was wagging. Must be good news.

"Good morning, Mr. Finnegan."

"Good morning to you, Miss Fox. To what do I owe the pleasure?"

"I have some good news for you. The Ministry of Equality just passed the Revolutionary Reparations Act. It awards reparations to those citizens whose ancestors were marginalized by the state, and penalizes those who benefited from that marginalization. Those citizens identified as marginalized will receive a percentage increase in wages, based on their historical degree of marginalization. Those citizens identified as marginalizers will have their wages garnished, based on the severity of ancestral tyranny."

Finbar wondered why this was good news for him.

He was a faun, after all. Fauns had never been marginalized or marginalizers. Historically, they'd mostly minded their own business.

"You have been categorized as marginalized," Miss Fox smiled.

"I have?" Finbar smiled back.

"You have. Ministry records indicate your great-great-great-grandmother on your mother's side was a pumpkin fairy. Isn't that great!"

Finbar gave the fox a puzzled stare. He'd had no idea that his great-great-great-grandmother on his mother's side was a pumpkin fairy, or what a pumpkin fairy even was. Miss Fox read the confused look on his face and explained.

"Pumpkin fairies are an extinct race of squash fairies from the Druidic Forest. Pumpkin fairies were hunted to extinction by tree elves, who murdered them for their eyeballs, which were made of particularly rare sapphire gemstones. Your great-great-great-grandmother was likely murdered, her priceless eyeballs plucked for profit."

"I—I—I had no idea..." Finbar was dumbfounded.

"Well, now you do. Expect your paycheck to be slightly larger next week in accordance with the reparations and your new marginalized status. Have a great day!"

"Great! You too."

Finbar shook his head in disbelief. What luck! He was pleased at the unexpected pay increase granted to him by the new legislation and his long-dead, great-great-great-pumpkin fairy grandmother. He wondered what a pumpkin fairy looked like, how much larger his paycheck might be, and if the pumpkin fairy genes had something to do with his carroty pubes.

-

Finbar spent much of the rest of that day at work researching stoicism. He found himself reading and re-reading the definition, trying to figure out why it was such a serious sin.

Stoicism was founded in ancient Athens by Zeno of Citium in the early 3rd century BC, but was famously practiced by the likes of Epictetus, Seneca, and Marcus Aurelius. According to its teachings, the path to happiness is found in accepting the moment as it presents itself, by not allowing oneself to be controlled by the desire for pleasure or fear of pain, by using one's mind to understand the world and to do one's part in nature's plan, and by working together and treating others fairly and justly. Stoicism doesn't concern itself with complicated theories about the world, but with helping people overcome destructive emotions and act on what can be acted upon. It's built for action, not endless debate.

Finbar didn't understand why such a philosophy would be illegal. In fact, stoicism sounded as decent and logical as any of the world's great religions. The more he learned, the more he liked.

The stoics believed that suffering largely emanates from within each person and that each person has the power to overcome suffering through conscious thought and learned habit.

The stoics realized that there are things we can control, and things we can't. To live a good life, individuals should focus on the things they can control and accept the rest as it happens. We can't change what already is, or has already occurred, but we can choose what to do with the given circumstances. Unhappiness is caused by the belief that we can control things we can't. We can't control the genes we were born with. We can't control all that happens to us. We can't control what the people around us say or do. We can't even fully control our own bodies, which get damaged and sick and ultimately die without regard for our preferences. The only thing that we really control is how we think about these things.

Finbar read on, failing to understand how such a philosophy could be considered even remotely sinful, let alone evil enough to be listed as one of the seven deadly isms. He consulted the Ministry of Equality's Holy Scriptures, where he found his answer within the

Revelations chapter of the Postmodern Testament.

The Ungodliness of Stoicism

From the First Apostle of Grievances

Victimhood is the most sacred principle of all postmodern catechism.

The most valiant are the most victimized. The most pious are the most persecuted. The most excellent are the most exploited. Sages must first be subjugated. Morality stems from and is learned from maltreatment.

The stoic is the anti-victim. Instead of encouraging victims to be defined by their victimhood, stoicism encourages them to ignore it, to rise above it. It encourages citizens to gain social status not by helplessness, but by strength and perseverance. Stoics do not indulge their injuries. They do not reward weakness. Stoics deny the holiness of victimhood, assuming themselves to be responsible for their own suffering, rather than society. They deny the fact that bigotry, racism, and sexism are endemic, insisting that victims of these crimes must use stoic thinking to endure.

Stoicism is an unholy philosophical concoction, meant to benefit only the rich and powerful. Stoicism gained popularity among the ancient elites because it was the one form of religious guidance that didn't encourage the redistribution of wealth and power to marginalized communities. Stoicism frowns upon changing the world outside ourselves, upon victim activism and resistance.

The following quote from Marcus Aurelius, Roman Emperor and stoic philosopher, demonstrates the deep-rooted evils of stoicism:

"Everything that happens is either endurable or not. If it's endurable, then endure it. Stop complaining. If it's unendurable... then stop complaining. Your destruction will mean its end as well. Just remember: you can endure anything your mind can make endurable, by treating it as in your interest to do so. In your interest, or in

your nature."

–

Later that same afternoon, Finbar was sipping his coffee, wishing it were wine and having conflicted thoughts on the sinfulness of stoicism. He was waiting for the five o'clock whistle when the creature resources manager returned. This time, her tail was not wagging. Must be bad news.

"Good afternoon, Finbar."

"Good afternoon, Miss Fox. To what do I owe the—"

"I have some bad news for you," she interrupted. "Your categorization has been changed from marginalized to marginalizer. We received updated government ancestral records, which indicate that your great-great-great-grandfather on your father's side was a rutabaga fairy."

Finbar gave the fox a puzzled stare. He'd had no idea that his great-great-great-grandfather on his father's side was a rutabaga fairy, or what a rutabaga fairy even was. Miss Fox read the confused look on his face and explained.

"Rutabaga fairies are an ancient race of cruciferous fairies from the Illusory Coast. They were among the first colonizers of Fantasmagoria. When they arrived, they mercilessly slaughtered the indigenous red elf tribes, decimating their coastal populations. Your great-great-great-grandfather was part of an especially diabolical rutabaga fairy colony, which authorized the deliberate use of disease-infested blankets as a biological weapon against a particularly defiant red elf tribe."

"I—I had no idea..." Finbar was dumbfounded, again.

"The Revolutionary Reparations Act has awarded the surviving red elf communities restitution for atrocities committed during the colonial period. Because you were found to be related, albeit distantly, to rutabaga fairies, your wages will be garnished starting next week. I'm so sorry!"

"B—b—b... But what about my other great-great-great-grandmother, the persecuted pumpkin fairy?" Finbar pleaded.

"According to the new law, all marginalized

identification is nullified by aggressor past. In other words, your pumpkin fairy ancestry is no longer acknowledged by the government."

"Oh."

"Sorry, I have to run. A tribunal is trying to behead a stone giant at five o'clock sharp. Should be quite the scene. Maybe I'll see you there? Oh, and have a great day!"

"Sure, sure. You too..."

Finbar was devastated. He wasn't exactly rich. No one at the newspaper was. Even a small garnishment to his paycheck would have real-life consequences for him.

Feeling poorer than ever, Finbar found himself reading through stoic teachings on wealth. The stoics viewed some level of wealth as necessary, but the relentless pursuit of it as a trap. Stoics believed the never-ending quest for wealth trapped the individual in a persistent state of want. In such a way, the rich became slaves to their own riches. Finbar happened upon an interesting quote on the subject.

"It is the privilege of the gods to want nothing, and of godlike men to want little."

The quote was by a former slave.

Ḣeroes Ṅo Ṁore

"Effective immediately, all branches of the military have been canceled by the Authority of Cancellation Culture, a newly created policy-making division of the Ministry of Equality."

Aristotle the grandfather clock read aloud from a newspaper behind the bar at the Tipsy Timepiece Tavern. Finbar sat nearby, sipping a hulking chalice of red wine. Fauns loved a hulking chalice of red wine. Took them back to good old days – the Cult of Dionysus days. The rest of the tavern was full. Everyone quietly listened to the stunning news.

"Findings from a recent diversity audit indicated

the military was toxically masculine, inherently imperialistic, and practicing in a range disability discriminations. Senior military commanders were also found guilty in the promotion of neocolonialism."

Aristotle turned the page. The bar was so quiet Finbar could hear the seconds ticking away on the old clock's face.

"All warriors of the Fantasmagorian military will be transitioned to social justice warriors. Service members will be redeployed throughout the kingdom to combat discriminative ideologies and promote equality. Battering rams, siege towers, catapults, personnel carriers, and all other combat support instruments will be scrapped. The timber from military equipment will be recycled into windmills to combat climate change. Naval vessels will be redirected to the South Sea to save endangered kraken. Swords, axes, and spears will be re-forged into silverware and tea sets for the needy."

The tavern gave a collective sigh.

"Wait, there's more..." Aristotle continued.

"Veteran's Day will be renamed Victim's Day.

Instead of honoring military veterans, the day will honor those many victims of military veterans. The military has played a strategic role in Fantasmagoria's shameful foreign policy, which has resulted in the enslavement and persecution of millions. The Department of Postcolonial Grievances will coordinate all Victim's Day celebrations."

A grizzled orc veteran who had been sitting next to Finbar drinking what looked very much like motor oil smashed his fist on the bar.

"Bollocks! Who do they expect will protect the kingdom from dragons, demons, dark dwarves, and death itself? Windmills? Kraken-saving warships? *Social justice warriors*? Dragons give all of zero shits about postcolonialism. Zero! Without knights patrolling the far reaches of Fantasmagoria, with *weapons*, a dragon holocaust is inevitable. Mark my words, it's just a matter of time—"

Just then, a troll walked into the bar. He was dressed in clothes that looked pulled straight from the closet of Jay Gatsby: a plain white-collared dress shirt, red suspenders, brown Oxford bag pants, and a felt top hat. He clenched a long, silver, full-bent pipe the size of a ladle in his teeth, which were hardly visible through his red walrus mustache. On his shoulder was a red, pentagonal-shaped endless knot patch—the symbol of the inquisition. He approached the bar, the whole tavern nervously watching.

"Good day. My name is Lucius. My preferred pronouns are lord, my lord, and his most virtuous lordship."

The bar stared at him.

"I identify as a royal, you see... We all have a right to be kings and queens."

The troll sat down at the bar across from the motor-oil drinking orc.

"Will his highness take something to drink this evening?" Aristotle asked, placing a coaster in front of the troll.

"Most certainly, my good grandfather clock. I am parched almost to death. It was a most tireless day of inquisiting. We raided a gender reveal party next door just hours ago. Nothing more transphobic than a group of cisgender bigots celebrating a baby's genitalia. How hateful it is for parents to presume a child's gender based on biological sex. How intensely hateful..."

"What will it be to drink, your majesty?"

"The drink, yes, of course. May I have a raspberry limoncello prosecco?"

"Nope."

"Nope! And why would that be?"

"No rasberries. No limoncello. No prosecco. Closest thing we have is a box of white wine." Aristotle lugged a mysterious-looking, warped box from under the bar. "What type of white wine it is I couldn't say for certain. There is no indication on the box. Will it suit your fancy?"

"I suppose it must."

Aristotle served the troll a glass of what looked like pond scum.

"Lord troll," the orc veteran barked from across the bar. "Your employer, the Ministry of Equality, has canceled the military. What say you to that?"

"I say good riddance to the military. That order of jugheads has enabled centuries of imperialistic, hyper-aggressive, and racist foreign policy. A postmodern military should be unarmed and emasculated. Our veterans should be publicly shamed for their long history of violence and oppression."

The orc's face turned a midnight shade of blue as it twisted with anger. The troll's face turned a slimy shade of green as it twisted with disgust—at the boxed wine.

The orc's voice rose, "Who will protect Fantasmagoria if not the military? What of marauders and monsters? What of the bloodthirsty barbarian hordes? What of dragons? *What of war*?"

"We live in an enlightened, globalized society," the troll replied calmly. "War is a thing of the past. A dragon has not been seen in years. Our greatest threats are internal. We must combat inequality and correct historical wrongs. The next generation of combatants will not wield swords; they will wield words. Social justice warriors are the hero crusaders whose holy mission it is to save Fantasmagoria from itself."

"Calling social justice warriors 'warriors' is an injustice to actual warriors. Calling them heroes is utter madness. The Ministry of Equality has canceled heroism. Your villains aren't even villains. They are ghosts of a long-dead past, one that is better forgotten than fought."

"Is that so?" The troll sipped the skunky wine, a menacing scowl on his face.

"It is. Do you know where heroes go when they get canceled?"

"No. Do tell."

"They go far away, somewhere you can't find them when you need them most. Someday, when Fantasmagoria needs real heroes to defend it—and it will—they will not come forth, because they will not believe this kingdom worth fighting for. Fantasmagoria will die defenseless, abandoned by its own righteousness."

The troll downed his white wine angrily.

"Would you like another glass, your highness?" Aristotle smiled.

The troll spat on the bar.

"I'd rather drink my own piss! I'll have this place boarded up before the week's end. I'll see every last one of you ride the Spanish donkey. Do you know who I am? DO YOU? I am a lieutenant to the grand inquisitor himself! I am an important troll! I am a—"

Suddenly, an ogre grabbed the troll by the neck and hurled him like a rag doll through the front bar window. Finbar looked out the broken window, watching and wondering if the troll was dead. He rose after a few seconds, shook his fist at the bar, then limped away.

The bar was silent for a few long seconds in collective shock, until someone broke the silence.

"The last hero of Fantasmagoria! Hip-hip-hooray!"

The whole tavern laughed and cheered, declaring the ogre famously brilliant. Aristotle the grandfather clock served up a celebratory round on the house. Finbar laughed and drank along with everyone else, but his was a worried laugh. The troll was an inquisitor, after all...

A Day at the Museum

Finbar loved the art museum almost as much as the Tipsy Timepiece Tavern. He loved it so much he was a member. *Premium* member, that is. Post-impressionist art was his favorite. Finbar considered himself an amateur post-impressionist art historian and collector of sorts. There were post-impressionist books, paintings, and reproductions stacked to the ceiling in his apartment. The art museum owned an extensive post-impressionist collection, which was one of the reasons Finbar spent so much time there.

One rainy Saturday, Finbar dropped by the museum. There was no line to get inside that day, which was unusual. There was always a line on weekends. At the admissions counter, Finbar presented his premium membership card to a troll that he didn't recognize, which was also unusual, for two reasons. Firstly, Finbar knew everyone who worked at the museum. Secondly, no trolls worked at the museum, or so he'd thought. There was more unusualness awaiting inside.

Finbar was surprised to find the floor plan of the museum totally changed. It seemed everything had been moved or replaced. A week before, he would have been able to find his favorite exhibits blindfolded. Now, he could hardly find the bathroom. He found himself wandering the museum for a long time, frustrated at not being able to find the post-impressionist works. As he wandered, he noticed much of the historical art had been replaced with modern art. The older the art was, the less likely it was to be found. Normally, the opposite would have been true.

The coffee shop was one of the few unchanged parts of the museum. While in line, Finbar recognized a curator named Shirley, with whom he was friendly. Shirley was an eccentric elf, who wore a high moss-colored stovepipe hat and riding habit, which made her look like a lost circus ringmaster. Finbar bought a coffee for each of them and sat down to catch up. He asked her why everything had been moved, and where it had been moved to.

"The museum *has* changed," Shirley whispered. "Has to do with new management."

"New management? I had no idea. Who might that be?"

"The Ministry of Equality." Shirley glanced around the coffee shop suspiciously. "They came in and turned this place upside down in a hurry. It all started with a big staff meeting last week, where some troll declared everyone here, including the art, not socially inclusive enough."

"*ART* is non-inclusive?"

"Apparently. The government is saying the

museum's collection did not meet modern, multicultural fine arts standards. Our new mission is not to display great works of art, but to engage disadvantaged communities. They established these new guidelines, where the art on display has to reflect the demographics of Fantasmagoria *exactly*."

"Which would explain why I can't find the post-impressionist collection," Finbar said disappointedly. "It was taking up a disproportionate amount of space given your new guidelines."

"Correct. We had to remove all but a few of the post-impressionist pieces to make room for more modern pieces. The post-impressionist exhibit was replaced with a postmodern digital art collection done by a blind trio of zombies. Let me just say, blind zombies don't make for the most talented artists in the realm. Also, the Ministry forced us to replace *The Thinker* sculpture with an eight-foot, bronze dildo from some sea monk expressionist no one has ever heard of. I thought it was a joke at first. Our best, most popular pieces are hiding in the basement!"

Finbar made a mental note to see the bronze dildo

statue.

"Renaissance art is getting an especially bad rap. Museum staff cannot refer to art from the period as 'renaissance art,' because the word 'renaissance' implies a period of humanistic and cultural progress. The Ministry is saying the renaissance should be viewed and referred to as a period of mass-slavery, religious intolerance, and artistic discrimination. The Ministry have required staff to use the phrase 'pre-modern arts' to refer to art from the period."

"If they're calling the renaissance intolerant, what are they calling everything before it?"

"Any art over six hundred years old has been canceled. Celtic, Carolingian, Gothic, Greek, Mesopotamian, Megalithic – it has all been removed from the floor. It's all hiding in the basement, and there are penalties for even looking at it. One of the exhibition assistants got caught sketching a copy of something Romanesque, so they plucked out his left eyeball and put it on display right where the Caesar statue was. Warning for the rest of the staff."

Finbar spat out a mouthful of coffee.

"Oh, and get this. They're renaming the museum. It won't be called a 'museum' anymore. It will be called The Inclusive Public Space for Non-Elitist Culture."

Finbar spat out another mouthful of coffee.

"Listen, Finbar it was great to catch up, but I need to run. I know you love the post-impressionist stuff. Most of it was canceled, but there is a little corner up on the top floor, across from the new exhibit on endangered jackalopes. You'll find some of what you came for up there."

"Thanks a million, Shirley. You be careful around here..."

"You too, Finbar..."

Finbar drank his coffee in a hurry, curious to see what remained of the museum's post-impressionist collection. He made his way to the main hall and up the museum's floating helical glass staircase, which was a work of art in its own right. Finbar stepped up, glad it was still there.

Arriving on the top floor, Finbar found the gallery empty. It was too quiet for comfort. Finbar could hear the rain pitter pattering on the roof. His footsteps made war on the silence, each one an explosion of echoes. He wondered if the floor wasn't closed entirely. Just then, a troll surprised him, emerging quickly from a side hall.

"May I help you?" the troll asked in an unhelpful tone.

"Err, yes. Post-Imp—" Finbar stopped, then corrected himself. "I mean jackalopes. The endangered jackelope exhibit... Where might that be?"

"Straight ahead, end of the hall on your right." The troll glared at Finbar. "Do avoid the pre-modern arts exhibit. It has been canceled until further notice."

Finbar proceeded to the jackelope exhibit, which was basically a grove of plastic trees. He pretended to admire the tree carvings and fossilized skeletons before sneaking across the hall to a dark corner, where the remnants of the museum's post-impressionist collection hung, along with a handful of other paintings.

There were a few paintings Finbar liked, but only one he loved – *The Scream*, by Edvard Munch. Finbar stared at the peculiar, panic-stricken screamer in the center of the painting for a long time. He stared until, by some strange illusion, he saw his own face in the screamer's. There he was, standing on the bridge beside the railing, tongues of flame and blood swirling above the whirling chaos of blue-black fjord behind him. Finbar opened his eyes and mouth as wide as he could, put his hands on the sides of his face, and felt what the screamer felt. He felt the infinite scream of insanity passing through Fantasmagoria. He felt it in the censorship, victimology, collectivism, conformity, ideological intolerance, identity politics, and government-forced belief systems. It was all amplified by the fear and division of the inquisition. The location of the painting itself was mad. It was on display in that unlit, pitiful corner of the museum, where the remnants of artistic masters had been relegated to make room for more socially inclusive art. He felt the insanity everywhere, and in everyone, even himself.

"Ahem." The same troll startled Finbar out of his trance. "This particular corner of the museum has been closed until further notice."

The troll escorted Finbar downstairs, past the

colossal bronze dildo. It was hideous. It was also the busiest exhibit in the museum. People were mad over the statue. They surrounded it, discussed it, took pictures with it, praised it. They worshipped it. Finbar wondered at the worshipping of giant dicks. It seemed to him the world had gone mad, and that fine art was canceled.

So, Finbar canceled his museum membership the next day.

In Which Finbar Authors an Article

Finbar arrived to work one morning surprised by the sight of Ivan the editor-in-chief seated in his chair, feet kicked up on the desk, wide grin glowing through his bushy blue beard.

"Finbar, Finbar, Finbar. It's a big, big, big day for

you, my goat-legged editorial assistant. Here in my furry hands I have your *very first* journalistic assignment."

Finbar was hardly able to contain himself. He'd been waiting for a real journalistic assignment his entire life. He couldn't wait to prove his worth as a writer, as a courageous journalist, as an indispensable asset to the *Elven Standard*. He couldn't wait to see his name in print. He wondered what his first assignment might be.

"Jeez. Thanks Ivan. What's the story? Is it the imp genocide in the northerly realms? Maybe the hobgoblin trafficking and orc slave trades emerging in developed kingdoms? Hobgoblin trafficking is not getting anywhere near enough attention in the media, if you ask me. A single story might save thousands of lives—"

"Those would all make for great stories I'm sure, but this is a business," Ivan interrupted. "Genocides and hobgoblin trafficking aren't selling papers these days. Our readers are looking for more personal, intersectional interest stories. The Ministry loves everything intersectional."

"Oh. Sure, sure..." Finbar nodded his head. He would've nodded his head to anything. He was happy just to have an actual writing assignment.

"Your first story is about an ogre. Well, he *was* an ogre. Now he's a gnome."

"How does an ogre become a gnome?" Finbar was genuinely confused.

"Great question. He *identifies* as a gnome, you see. Still looks very much like an ogre. Now, a transracial ogre wouldn't itself be newsworthy, but there's more. Turns out this particular transracial ogre just won the power-lifting world title in the gnomish division. Caused a little bit of controversy, you know with him being a shit-kicking ogre and what not. He ended up smashing every gnome power-lifting record in the books, as you'd expect."

Ivan stood up and handed Finbar a manila envelope.

"Details are all in here. Take a read through and draft me up something inspirational. We need this to be a feel-good story about the transracial community overcoming adversity. We need this ogre, or gnome, or whatever in witch's tits he wants to call himself, to be the hero. Fantasmagoria readers adore a modern, marginalized hero."

Ivan patted Finbar on the back and walked away. Finbar opened the manila envelope and read through the details. It wasn't the sort of first assignment he had expected. Or wanted. Still, it *was* an assignment. If he did his best, maybe management would notice. Maybe he would get an opportunity for a bigger, more meaningful story.

Finbar wondered how to put a hero spin on the whole thing as he scribbled an outline for the article. An ogre winning a gnome power-lifting competition? Seemed unfair at best, maybe even preposterous. Finbar didn't consider the ogre-turned-gnome a hero. Still, he had to make him one. A job was a job, and he was on the payroll. So, he got to typing.

Transracial Gnome Breaks Racial Barriers

In a brave and beautiful story from the world

of competitive power-lifting, a former mountain ogre named Rog Stein (formerly Azrog Steinmeintz) who identifies as a gnome, has been crowned the strongest gnome in the world, winning gold at the World Power-Lifting Championships in the fiercely competitive gnomish division.

In the final round of the tournament, the transracial hero deadlifted an astonishing 5,650 pounds, beating the second-place contender by 5,625 pounds. With his incredible lift, Stein also annihilated the previous gnomish deadlifting record of 28.5 pounds.

The Elven Standard interviewed the world champion to discuss his transition from ogre to gnome and his newfound success as a gnomish power-lifter.

"I may look like an ogre on the outside, but on the inside, I'm all gnome. I've always felt more myself in much smaller-sized clothing. I'm a huge fan of those colorful, pointy hats. I even refused to eat gnome-meat growing up. Tried it once, and *it felt like cannibalism. Honestly. It's true I never power-lifted when I was an ogre, but it felt like the right thing to do after my transition to gnome. I wanted to bring more attention to the cause of transracials like me. It takes real courage to be who you were born to be, especially when that happens to be a gnome and you happen to have been born in the body of a seven-hundred-pound mountain ogre."*

Critics claim Stein had an unfair advantage in the competition, due to his sheer size and having once been an ogre. Stein explained that any advantage he had was diminished from the transracial hormonal therapy he receives on a weekly basis, which has changed many of his physical characteristics from ogrish to gnomish, while also significantly reducing his overall muscle mass.

That explanation did not satisfy everyone. One gnomish power-lifter was arrested by the Ministry of Equality for protesting the competition result. The gnome has been charged with bigotry and banned for life from competitive power-lifting. He is scheduled to be tried in court for his crimes next Friday afternoon. The penalty for bigotry is death by burning.

Congratulations to Rog Stein, our newest national hero.

~ Finbar Finnegan, Associate Journalist

-

Finbar walked home from work that day. It was a fine day for walking. There were no public torturings or executions to speak of. Not a cloud in the sky. That end of summer sun shone pale and the early autumn wind blew up a leafy gale. Finbar walked and the weather was so nice he hoped he had farther to walk.

As it was a windy day, **Finbar** encountered that mysterious old man who only appeared outside when the winds blew. He sat on the front steps of his house, still as the blonde bungalow bricks behind him. Finbar might have mistaken him for a statue were it not for the breeze blowing back his long white hair. He looked how he always did. His eyes were calmly closed, and he wore that same mischievous smile. Finbar walked up to introduce himself, hoping to learn the secret of the old man and the wind.

"Hullo there, sir. Name's Finbar Finnegan. Mighty glad to meet you."

Finbar bowed his horns and held out his hand, but the old man didn't move. Not a muscle. The smile on his face was unmoving. His eyes remained shut, though clearly moving under the lids, as if he were awake in some deep dream world.

"Excuse me, sir. You there?"

The old man wasn't there. He was somewhere else entirely. It was as though he was hypnotized by the wind, or entranced by some other invisible magic.

There wasn't much more Finbar could do except to continue on his way, wondering what hypnotic spell the wind cast on the old man. When he reached his apartment, he opened all his windows, inviting the wind in. It was a warm wind. There was no reason to keep it out. Finbar fell asleep to the ruffling of leaves high in the trees outside his window. He dreamt of transracial wind spirits powerlifting the sun.

The Turn of the

Screw

Finbar was passing through the marketplace one ordinary day when he noticed something out of the ordinary. A sandy-haired goblin sat in what looked like an electric chair as he was tried for inquisition-related crimes. He wore an odd-looking metal crown that had screws with levers extending from each side by the ears. A plate sat below the goblin's jaw that was connected by a frame to the metal crown. Finbar had never seen such a device. It made him curious. He stopped to watch the proceedings, joining the swelling crowd of spectators. A hatchet-faced troll stood on a raised wooden platform, reading aloud the charges.

"Sir goblin, you stand before this holiest of tribunals accused of hate speech against vampires. Inquisition evidence indicates that you once used a derogatory term for vampires. In a private, hand-written letter you sent to a friend approximately four hundred and seventy-two years ago, you used the phrase *'corpse humper'* to describe a vampire…"

Scattered giggles sounded from the crowd.

"Ahem… As you know, vampires are a protected class in Fantasmagoria. Usage of speech intended to demean or degrade protected classes is considered hate speech, and a severe crime."

"It was a JOKE!" the goblin yelled, because of course it was. Finbar knew it was a joke. The tribunal knew it was a joke. Everyone knew it was a joke. That didn't matter.

"Joke or no joke, it matters not. All jokes against protected classes, or jokes deemed even remotely offensive by protected classes, are highly illegal. Jokes were made illegal by the Ministry of Equality ex post facto, meaning your joke, though legal when you first made it, has now been criminalized and may (and will) be prosecuted to the fullest extent by this tribunal."

"*It was four hundred and seventy-two years ago!*" the goblin wailed.

"The statute of limitations for offensive jokes is seven thousand four hundred twenty-two years. Even if the joke were beyond the statute of limitations, we would uphold the charge. This tribunal was recently informed of another hateful crime committed by you. We have additional evidence here, submitted by your elementary school principal, which indicates you once played 'Smear the Queer,' a game in which the player with the football is labeled 'queer' and assaulted by the other players. Do you deny participating in this hateful, homophobic game?"

The goblin rose from the electric-looking chair in protest. A mountainous mountain troll forced him back down by the shoulders. The goblin opened his mouth, but no words came out. There was no point. He resigned himself to his fate.

"This tribunal would ask for your repentance for these heinous crimes, but it would do you no good. Crimes of past hate speech have never, and will never, be forgiven by the Ministry of Equality. Vampires are not corpse humpers. Furthermore, jokes about corpse humpers are far more illegal than actual corpse humping. Vampires are well-meaning and productive members of society. You should be ashamed of yourself."

The troll paused for dramatic effect.

"This tribunal sentences you to death by head crushing. After your sentence is carried out, your blood will be donated to the Front Street Vampire Orphanage, where it will help to nourish those vampires most in need during the holiday season. Do you have any last words?"

The goblin breathed in deeply, then started sobbing. After a few seconds, the sob turned into a hysterical laughter. After he was all cried and laughed out, he cleared his voice.

"What do you call a gay vampire?"

The crowd fell silent with interest.

"A fruit bat!"

Scattered giggles sounded throughout the crowd as a group of trolls swarmed the goblin, tying his legs and wrists to the chair. Once he was secured, all the trolls backed away, except for one who was wearing a black butcher's apron – the executioner. The executioner turned a screw on one side of the metal crown device. He turned it ever so slowly and carefully.

Except for a hardly noticeable tremble, the goblin stayed perfectly still in the chair, eyes closed. After a few turns of the screw, the goblin slowly opened his eyes, or the machine opened them for him. The more the troll turned the screw, the wider the goblin's eyes opened. The troll turned and turned the device, the goblin's eyes opening wider and wider, until it seemed they could open no wider. Then the troll turned the screw once more. The goblin squealed as his eyeballs shot from their sockets into the crowd like little red pebbles.

The crowd let out a collective shriek. Some of those closest to the head crushing vomited. Finbar stood there, unable to move, paralyzed with shock.

Most of the crowd was that way. No one cheered, or moved, they just stood there like a massive exhibit of dazed sculptures.

The executioner resumed the turning of the screw and chunks of brain began gushing out of the goblin's eye sockets, blood streaming forth from his nose like an out of control faucet. He continued turning the device until he couldn't turn it anymore. The lever attached to the screw was stuck. More trolls gathered around, all pushing the lever together. When it did finally come unstuck, it let out a horrendous crack as the goblin's jaw broke. Shattered teeth flew from his mouth like bloody buckshot. The troll turned the screw another few times, until another louder crack was heard, this time the skull. By the time the troll had finished, the goblin's head looked like tomato puree.

The crowd snapped out it, turning away from the traumatic scene, going back to the business of the day. Finbar blinked stupidly at the afternoon sun blazing behind the platform where a troll stood to address the remnants of the crowd. What else could he possibly have to say?

"Comedy is canceled..." the troll laughed.

Only he wasn't joking.

The River of

Deceit

Finbar might have been employed as an editorial assistant, but he was an outdoorsman at heart. He liked the woodsy scent of a campfire, the sound of rain on a tent flap, the sight of a cockatrice flying wild. Like so many, he felt most at peace in the wilderness. With the inquisition raging, he needed peace more than ever. So, one weekend he decided to go camping.

Finbar left the office late one morning, arriving at camp later in the afternoon. He camped in a deep, secluded corner of the Druidic Forest, far from the hustle and bustle of the city. He pitched his tent on a grassy knoll overlooking a glade so white with daisies you'd have mistaken them for a fresh blanket of snow. The glade was important, and not just for the daisies. Above it, the night sky shone, free from light pollution, smog, and all traces of civilization. That unobstructed, star-studded yonder cured Finbar of commerce. It cured him every single time.

After he pitched his tent, Finbar got a modest fire going. The plan was to cook dinner, then go for a night hike to the River of Deceit, a mystical river that flowed through the heart of the forest. It was called the River of Deceit because of the enchanted source. It was said the river rose and fell with all the collective lies of Fantasmagoria. When it flowed low and slow, truth and justice prevailed in the kingdom. When it flowed high and swift, lies were the cause. Finbar had heard rumors the river was running wild. He wanted to see for himself.

-

Finbar set forth at dusk, bringing only a lantern

with him. A gust of wind surprised him as he started across the glade toward the river trail. Dark clouds gathered overhead. Forked lightning pierced the horizon, joined by a grumble of thunder from not so far-away. That earthy scent of rain filled the air. A storm left over from summer was on the way. Finbar hurried along, the rain holding off until he was under the trees, so he was mostly sheltered from it as he made his way through the woods.

Finbar wasn't far along the trail when a crosswind breached the thin glass case of his lantern, blowing out the candle and leaving him quite in the dark. He hiked more slowly after that, careful not to lose his way. The trail snuck cleverly around trees and bushes, over creeks and glens, under bridges and boulders, keeping on steadily toward the river. Lightning flashed more frequently the further he walked, at times helping him to navigate the path, at other times exposing the gnarled, ghoulish faces of the trees who stared angrily at him as he passed them by. The forest was unwelcoming that night.

Walking on, Finbar heard the flow of the river

between the sound of the blowing trees and the rain and knew he was close. The trail climbed steeply at its end. He had reached the hilly boundary of the woods that separated it from the river when he noticed a warning carved into a wide tree trunk.

Danger

Truth Turn Around
Liars Don't Drown

Finbar didn't turn around. He'd come too far to turn around. He reached the end of the trail and looked down onto the river. At first, it was indistinguishable from the rainy night sky. But when his eyes adjusted to the distance and darkness, he saw it.

The river was far wider than Finbar had ever seen it. It looked more ocean than river. It heaved with lies. Finbar could see them—deceitful apparitions splashing and screaming in the currents like maniacal skinny-dippers. He saw politicians, priests, and professors turned sea serpents. He saw tribunals of vampire squids trying inquisition cases. Splashes and waves transformed into the tentacles of a monstrous kraken, engulfing heretics. The liars walked on water. The honest drowned in it. Occasionally, a lightning flash would rend the sky from top to bottom, unleashing electrical demons throughout the air, who joined in the mayhem. The waters roared with the sound of laughter and lies. Rain poured, thunder rolled, and lightning struck, the now full-blown storm adding to the otherworldly scene.

Finbar was hypnotized by the treacherous mayhem. He stood there on the hill, soaking wet, looking down over the raging river haunted with lies. It was hard to say how long he stood there for. If he could have recounted minutes as they pass in a nightmare, he might have known. It was likely quite long, because he was eventually spotted by a band of river trolls.

They approached from the opposite bank, walking on the cursed waters as only true liars could. Finbar didn't notice them until they were about halfway across the river. The waters settled down, the current slowing and clearing a path for them, as if by their command. Glowing gold troll eyes shone on the water like ominous floating candles. They were coming straight for him.

Finbar dashed back into the woods down the trail.

"Hey you, faun! Halt! IN THE NAME OF THE INQUISITION HAAAALT!"

Finbar heard the trolls shouting at him as they splashed out of the river, swarming after him down the trail. He galloped away as fast as he could, but the trolls were faster. He could hear them gaining on him. They were nearly upon him when the trail veered sharply and he found himself out of his pursuers line of sight for a few seconds. Seizing the opportunity, he dove off the trail into a dark, leaf-filled ditch. He lay there as still as could be, watching the troop of trolls race by him at a ferocious speed.

It was many minutes before Finbar dared move a muscle. He lay there, convulsing from the cold rain and fear, teeth chattering, heart bulging from out of his furry chest. He wondered what crime he had committed, and what so many trolls were doing in the middle of nowhere. Why were they guarding the River of Deceit? It must have had something to do with the overflow. Perhaps the trolls were a security detail for lies. Lies must be guarded, lest they escape.

Finbar didn't take the same trail back for fear of encountering the band of trolls. He decided it best to cut through the pathless forest. He army-crawled across the trail, then rolled down the opposite bank and into the woods below, making for the general direction of his campsite. The forest was nearly pitch black. All Finbar could see between the trees were scattered pillars of lightning shining through chinks in the leaves above. The trees and undergrowth were thicker and more tangled than they appeared, so he didn't get on very fast, but he found his way.

He was exhausted by the time he returned to his campsite much later that night. Tired as he was, he couldn't sleep. He lay in his tent, listening to the sound of the rain on his tent flap. He no longer liked the sound of rain on a tent flap. It kept him awake. The pitter-patter sounded too much like the footsteps of trolls along a trail.

So much for a weekend getaway.

A Ghost Walks

into a Bar

It was one of those dark and stormy nights you're always hearing about—the perfect night for a ghost to walk into a bar. Stray patches of fog creeped up and down the drenched city streets like roaming clumps of spirits. The eyes of passersby glowed like will-o-the-wisps beneath the shadows of umbrellas. Barren trees came to life, dancing like berserk gingerbread men in the wind. The night was utterly ghostly, and the Tipsy Timepiece Tavern was due for a haunting.

Finbar had come in dripping wet from the storm and been served a warm blanket by Aristotle. He was drying himself near the fireplace when he saw the ghost sitting nearby. Finbar could tell straight away he was a ghost. His silver hair looked like smoke woven through the glowing circlet on his head. He cast no shadow from the roaring fire. His skin was more apparition than anything. He looked like the ghost of a middle-aged valley elf.

The ghost nodded a hello to Finbar from across the room, his lifeless eyes twinkling with curiosity. The ghost wasn't the least bit scary. In fact, he looked friendly. And familiar. Finbar wondered if he hadn't met him before.

"Can I get you a drink?" Finbar hollered over, wondering what ghosts drank.

"No thanks. They say spirits drinking spirits is bad luck. It's a form of supernatural cannibalism."

The ghost joined Finbar nearer to the fire.

"My throat *is* parched with the dust of death. I'd die—again—for a porter."

Finbar fetched a creamy pitcher of porter for

himself and the ghost, threw a log on the fire, and got to talking.

"Can't say I've ever met a ghost. May I ask how you got in the ghosting business?"

"Of course. I got in the ghosting business the usual way. Inquisition. Torture. I was charged with excessive excellence. Died of a compliment! I rode the infamous Spanish donkey not three weeks ago, up in the great meadow on the outskirts of town. It was quite the ordeal, or so I hear. I don't remember much, thank heavens."

Finbar realized then that he was talking to the ghost of the very same valley elf he'd seen tortured to death on the Spanish donkey. He didn't let on that he'd been a spectator. Might prove awkward.

"Probably better not to remember, eh?" Finbar clanked glasses with the ghost, who nodded in agreement. "Being a ghost, you must have more than a few ghost stories. Here we are, sitting by the fire, the storm storming outside. These are ideal conditions for a ghost story. You go first."

An expectant crowd swelled around the fireplace.

The ghost made quite the show of it, levitating over the fireplace mantel, drink in hand, holding court until late into the night. He told stories of banshee wails heralding the deaths of kings, and of their roaming ghosts haunting barren castles. He described devourers of the dead, soul swallowers, headless horseman, ladies in white, ladies in red, and every other sort of specter you could imagine. There were ghost ships haunting the high seas, vanishing hitchhikers vanishing in the back seat, murdered peddlers selling housewares, and plenty more along those lines. The crowd couldn't get enough. Nothing like ghost stories from a primary source. Makes them all the more credible.

Eventually the stories ended, but the porter didn't. Ghost stories from the dead put everyone in the drinking mood. Aristotle could hardly keep up. The alcohol was flowing like the River of Deceit. Finbar was putting them back like a half-goat Winston Churchill. He talked until midnight with the ghost, who seemed in no hurry to leave, and who drank a respectable fill himself.

"What brings a ghost out tonight?" Finbar wondered why he hadn't asked the question sooner.

"Why, didn't you know? There are ghosts haunting every nook and cranny of the kingdom tonight. The Ministry of Equality dug up the whole damned city graveyard!"

"What! Why would they do that?"

"Discrimination of the dead."

"Discrimination of the who? Are you serious?"

"*Dead* serious, pun intended. The Ministry of Equality recently conducted a study of the tombstones in the graveyard. The purpose of the study was to ensure that all the different classes of deceased were equally represented in the cemetery. They measured and weighed a sample of graves, finding the male graves to be consistently taller and heavier than the female graves. There is a massive grave replacement project underway, intended to make the graveyard less sexist by reducing the average size of the male graves and making them equal in size to the female graves."

"A sexist graveyard... That is without question the most absurd tale these ears have heard. So, let me get this straight, you were dug out of your own grave?"

"Sort of. I lived in a mausoleum, along with the rest of my ancestors. The government bulldozed the whole thing to the ground. Left us all homeless, or graveless, for the time being."

"How—how awful?"

"Well yes, awful in that they've haunted the whole city. Digging up graves comes with a certain supernatural risk. The Ministry should have taken the advice on Will Shakespeare's grave:

> *Good friend for Jesus sake forbeare,*
> *To dig the dust enclosed here.*
> *Blessed be the man that spares these stones,*
> *And cursed be he that moves my bones.*

"On the other hand, being dug out of your own grave is not the end of the world. It's more a resuscitating of it. It feels fine to get out on the town on my own, you know, to have a drink and have a normal conversation like this. Try spending an eternity with the entirety of your dead family. It's not all shits and giggles."

Finbar and the ghost were the last ones at the bar that night. Finbar was drunk as a faun fiddler. So was the ghost. At the end of it all, Finbar drank what was left from his glass and proceeded to the jukebox. He barely made it there. The room was spinning, but he managed to drop a coin in. The bar was so quiet, **the coin echoed like a tear in the fabric of time as it tumbled through the slot.** Finbar leaned on the music machine, clinging to consciousness, waiting for his song to play. The last thing he remembered was the ghost, snorting pixie dust off the bar. Aristotle laughed at them both until the song came on, drowning everything else out.

>*If there's something strange*
>*In your neighborhood*
>*Who you gonna call...*

By Today's

Standards

Finbar was a voracious reader. His appetite for books was as insatiable as his appetite for fine wine. His literary tastes were expansive. He read everything—fiction, non-fiction, fantasy, history, historical fantasy, poetry, even gnomic poetry. He owned a respectable collection of his own books, but had lately been sourcing most of his titles from the local library. The reparations garnishment had hit his wallet hard. He was trying to save money wherever possible.

One day, Finbar dropped by his local library for some fresh meat.

The moment he walked through the library doors he sensed something was off. It wasn't that anything looked different. It was the smell. A library has a distinct smell—that earthy, decomposing story scent. Finbar loved that smell. He stood there, drinking the library air in deep, feeling calm and glad, until he noticed the smell was less potent. Less bookish. There was a tinge of something else in the air, something too crisp for a library.

Finbar set forth through the aisles. He had just finished something historical, so was in the mood for something fantastical. He planned on choosing from the library's Tolkien collection. *The Hobbit* was his all-time favorite. Something with a Baggins was always in the reading rotation. So, he was understandably mortified when he found that all evidence of Middle Earth had vanished from the library. He found a librarian, who explained to him the situation.

"The Ministry of Equality has begun circulating an

Index of Forbidden Books to all libraries in Fantasmagoria," the librarian whispered quieter than a library voice. "It lists books banned for ideologically imperfect or heretical content. The first list we received removed everything from Tolkien. I believe it was categorized as culturally biased, possibly even racist."

"You're kidding..."

"Unfortunately, no. The mostly white, elvish good guys of Middle Earth doing battle with the legions of darker-skinned orcs was interpreted as racist, and that wasn't all. Hobbits were believed to be represented as racially inferior due to their smaller stature and pot bellies. The fact there was no female representation whatsoever in the wizardry class was, of course, problematic. Aragorn was thought to be styled as a fascist dictator. The fact there isn't a single queer character in a thousand plus pages is likely what doomed it..."

Finbar wondered to himself if Sam and Frodo weren't gay. They sure acted like it.

"I'm sorry, Finbar. There were plenty of other

popular authors banned. Shakespeare, Lovecraft, Lewis Carroll. Just last week, the Ministry made us burn every Dr. Seuss book we had in stock, along with any book associated with or inspired by Dr. Seuss. None of those old books pass equitable muster nowadays. Half of our best-selling authors were found to be heretics by today's standards."

By today's standards.

Finbar thought about that. It seemed ridiculous to judge yesterday by today's standards. To penalize the past in the present suggested that the kingdom was better today, or would have known better than all those who came before them. Would they really have known better? Finbar didn't think so, and it seemed arrogant to think so. The only reason the kingdom thought they would have known better was because they knew the full story of the past. People living in the past didn't know how that story would end. They made the decisions they made, given the commonly held beliefs of the time, for right or wrong. They believed the earth was flat because it was taught in schools. They believed golems were racially inferior because it was church canon. They believed what *was* believed, not what was necessarily true. Learning the truth takes a lifetime. Teaching it takes ages. For that reason, the past should be exonerated, at least to some degree. Unfortunately for the library and Finbar, the Ministry of Equality didn't believe in exoneration.

Finbar perused the rest of the fantasy shelves, hoping to happen upon something else he might like. He had no such luck. Most of the books appeared brand new, likely replacements for all the older, banned books. There was a disproportionate number of titles focusing on the spectrum of sexuality, gender, and race. There were far, far too many vampire romances. He made his way to the history shelves. He was sure to find something there.

The history shelves were completely empty. A sign was all that was left.

History Banned Until Further Notice

History is written by the victors. Unfortunately, the victors were lying, racist, heteronormative imperialists. The Ministry of Equality recently reviewed a sample of library-owned history books and found them to be bloated with ethnocentric and inaccurate narratives. White, elven scholars and historians have sustained these fallacious histories for far too long. The Ministry of Equality is conducting a thorough rewriting of all history. History will be written not by the winners, but by the losers. It will be written not as a story of progress, but as one of tragedy. Royal fairytales will be replaced with slavery narratives. Kings and queens will be judged not by their successes, but by their failures. Heroes will be re-identified. Jesus Christ will be a genderqueer djinn. Leonardo DaVinci will be a thimble fairy. Abraham Lincoln will be a transsexual hobgoblin. And so on. The new history of Fantasmagoria will be an all-inclusive history, one we can all be proud of. It will be a history without mistakes to be forgive, because the Ministry of Equality does not forgive mistakes.

Finbar disappointedly returned to the fiction shelves, though it seemed to him the history shelves might soon be indistinguishable from the fiction shelves. Oh well. At least there were books left on the shelves here and there. He was bound to find something.

Returning to fiction Finbar looked for *Peter Pan*, but there was no sign of the original. Probably banned for its stereotypical Indian depiction, he guessed. There were, however, *Peter Pan* retellings on the shelves. Finbar flipped through the pages of an erotic, progressive take of the story, one in which Captain Hook and Peter fall in love. Smee officiates their wedding on Skull Rock. The pirates are assimilated into the Piccaninny tribe. Tiger Lily is declared the empress of Neverland. The Lost Boys are adopted by Pan and Hook, joining them on the *Jolly Roger*, which sails off into the sunset. Everyone grows up, even Peter.

Finbar was unimpressed. He settled on one of the hundreds of vampire romances.

It was god awful.

-

With no stories worth reading, Finbar made his way to the Tipsy Timepiece, where he hoped to hear a story worth telling. The tavern was quiet that evening, with only a handful of elves seated around a corner table drinking from an immense, genie-shaped bottle of something sparkling. Some stout-looking—and drinking—goblins sat in another corner. A tired and/or drunk gnome slept on the fireplace mantel. Finbar bellied up to the bar and began chatting with Aristotle.

"You know about the old man in the wind?" Finbar asked Aristotle. "He's that peculiar fella lives on my block in that beautiful, blonde brick bungalow. He only ever comes out in a steady breeze. When he does, he just sits there on his porch in a sort of trance. I swear it's the strangest thing you ever saw."

"Is it strange? The wind can take you places, if only you close your eyes and listen closely to it." Aristotle smiled knowingly.

"Well go on, tell me what I don't know. Tell me the old man's story."

"Can't. Some stories can only ever be told by those that lived 'em. The old man's story is one of those. You'd have to go ask him to tell it. He'd be willing."

"I've tried. The old man can't be bothered when he's out in the wind. As I said, it's like he's in some sort of trance."

"Ah, now that I can help you with. The old man was once a seaman. All you need is a pinch of sea salt. Sea salt is like a smelling salt for retired mariners. It would wake them from the dead. Let me peek around down here see if I have any left. Used to use it for a fishy cocktail..."

Aristotle searched the bar top to bottom for that pinch of sea salt. He looked under the bar, over the bar, behind the bar, until he finally found it *on* the bar, tucked sneakily between a row of coasters. It was a seemingly ordinary salt packet, with 'sea' printed on it. He handed it to Finbar.

"There you go. That wee bit of sea salt would wake the ghost of Davy Jones himself. Next time you see the old man in the wind, walk up and waft a bit of those crystals under his nose. He'll awaken from the spell in no time."

"Spell?"

"Yes, spell. Finish that there draft and find the old man in the next one."

There wasn't a draft that day, but the next time there was, Finbar intended to do just that.

Diversity and Plaguery

Elven Standard management sat worriedly around a conference room table. They had good reason to be worried. They were being audited by the Ministry of Equality. It was a dreaded equality audit, meant to ensure perfectly equal levels of racial and sexual representation within the company. Finbar the editorial assistant sat at the foot of the table, taking notes. Ivan the editor-in-chief stood at the head of the table, speaking.

"*Bad* news folks! Turns out, our diversity numbers are not diverse. And, if we don't make them diverse, the Ministry of Equality will make them diverse for us. The Ministry's means of forced employee diversification? Burning at the stake. Beheading. Hanging. Take your pick…"

Ivan pointed to a mishmash of colorful pie charts hanging on the wall behind him, which contained the legally required breakdown of employees by race, gender, sexual orientation, and more. The largest chart contained a perfectly equal distribution of elves, goblins, dwarves, trolls, gnomes, fairies, as well as an 'other' category which included fauns, mermaids, wyverns, and more. Ivan pointed to the charts.

"Here are the new diversity quotas needed to pass the audit."

Everyone processed the pie charts in confused silence, until an elf spoke up.

"I see the term 'polyracial' in the ethnic identity chart. What does polyracial mean?"

Everyone in the meeting shook their head and murmured, looking even more confused.

"Hell if I know." Ivan fingered his beard nervously. "Finbar, any idea?"

Finbar flipped through the *Ministry of Equality Guide to Identity,* where he found the definition and read it aloud.

"The polyracial community identifies as many different races, either simultaneously or varying between those races. For example, an elf may identify as both a fairy and goblin, or a fairy one week and a goblin the next. Polyracial citizens may also identify as polygender or gender fluid, which describes any person whose gender identity varies over time."

Everyone in the meeting looked even more confused. Ivan paced slowly around the table.

"Dwarves like me, we're the real problem. The fact of the matter is we employ a disproportionate number of dwarves. Half the whole staff writer department are dwarves. The mail room has more dwarves than mail. Even the janitor is a dwarf. We've literally got dwarves falling out of the goddamned windows. With these new diversity quotas, we'll have no choice but to lay off a good chunk of them. I'll have to fire myself!"

The dwarves in the room frowned grumpily until one spoke up.

"Say we do lay off half the dwarves that work here. We still won't meet the full diversity quota. Our sexual orientation figures are ass backwards. Without half the newspaper coming out of the closet as gay, lesbian, or trans, there's no way we'll hit our numbers."

Ivan tucked his beard into his belt and sat down. "Well, anyone have any ideas?"

Thumbs twiddled hopelessly around the conference room table. No one had any idea how the quota could be met without re-staffing the entire newspaper, top to bottom. Finbar was flipping curiously through the identity guide, reading through all the unusual identities, when one caught his eye.

Pansexual: Also known as omni-sexual, pansexuals have a gender-blind sexual orientation, and are open to relationships with those who do not identify with one gender, race, or sexual preference.

"Ahem, Ivan. I have an idea."

"What is it Finnegan?"

"Pansexuals."

"Pan-what-uals?"

"Pansexuals. Pansexuals can have multiple sexual preferences at the same time."

"SO?"

"So, it seems to me that if we hire one pansexual, we just might be able to count that employee as gay, lesbian, straight, and trans. As far as the audit is concerned, that's four for the price of one."

"Go on." Ivan stroked his beard thoughtfully.

"Unless I'm mistaken, the same theory applies to polyracials. If we found a polyracial, we'd be able to count them as being more than one race in the equality audit. And if we found a polyracial pansexual, we could count them for virtually everything. Theoretically, we could a hire a single employee that could be counted as gay, lesbian, goblin, faun, dwarf, elf, fairy and more. We'd only need to hire a handful of these employees to pass the audit with flying colors."

"Finbar Finnegan, you're a blasted GENIUS!"

The entire room stood up and applauded. Finbar blushed.

"Alright, alright, settle right down, folks. We're not out of the diversity woods yet. We still have work to do. Creature resources, track down the resumes of as many polyracial pansexuals as possible. I want more polyracial pansexuals hired here than I know what to do with. Pay them a FUCK TON, that way we can represent equality in salaries across employee demographics. While you're at it, tell the dwarves in the mailroom they can declare themselves polyracial, pansexual, or unemployed. I'll do the same. As of now, I'm officially an anthropomorphic, bisexual pygmy. After we've made the employee identity changes, go right ahead and promote every single minority on staff. And freeze hiring to all overrepresented races. And I mean *all* hiring. I don't care if Ernest fucking Hemingway applies for a staff writer job here. We're not hiring him if he's worsening our diversity score. Let's also hire a diversity analyst. That's a progressive move. We'll need someone to manage these diversity audits going forward and to make sure we're operating within acceptable diversity standards. Anyone have any questions?"

"One more thing, sir," a bespectacled goblin uttered. "According to the audit, we're required by law to have a chief creature officer on staff."

"Oh, great. What in witch's tits does a chief creature officer do?"

Finbar thought he heard a cricket. Ivan pointed at Finbar.

"Congratulations, Finnegan. You've just been promoted to chief creature officer..."

-

"Next order of business..." Ivan shuffled through some documents on the table. "What's the next order or business again? Someone? Anyone?"

"The new plague, sir," Finbar pointed out.

"The new plague indeed! Hottest story we've had since the old plague."

Ivan cleared his throat for an old song:

I had a little bird, her name was Enza.
I opened up the window, and in-flu-Enza.

Ivan bowed to soft claps around the table. "Thank you, thank you. Give us the latest on this newest plague, young Finnegan. What do we know of it?"

"Symptoms are mild, generally cold and flu-like for the majority of the infected, but for an unlucky few it progresses to pneumonia and kills. We're not sure where it came from, but right now it's concentrated in the Oriental End, and seems to be spreading in a hurry. There is no treatment to speak of."

"*Who* is it killing, exactly? That's the important question."

"We're seeing much higher death rates within the ogre, imp, and curvy mermaid populations. Those groups tend to have higher rates of the underlying conditions which exacerbate the plague – things like obesity, diabetes, and high blood pressure."

"Sounds like a racist plague to me?" Ivan posed the question to the table. Everyone looked at each other in confusion. Miss Fox from creature resources said what everyone was thinking.

"How can a plague be racist?"

"It can't. We're making it racist. Why? Racist plagues sell newspapers better than non-racist plagues. I can see the headline now."

"Racial Pandemic Wreaks Havoc"

"We need to make this story less about biology and more about inequality. I don't want reporting on the medical reasons someone with glucose intolerance has a weakened immune system. I want glucose intolerance to be the direct result of structural racism within our government, or the marketing of unhealthy foods to disadvantaged communities. Make all of those pre-existing conditions socioeconomic as opposed to scientific. Make high blood pressure prejudiced. Make diabetes intolerant. Our readers will buy that."

The table took notes. Finbar tried, but had a guilty feeling forming in the pit his stomach.

"Ivan, wouldn't it be more responsible of the newspaper to publish some sort of call to action for *all* citizens of Fantasmagoria to improve their own health and take personal responsibility for their own well-being? Wouldn't that be more helpful to our readers, and the kingdom as a whole, than publishing blame narratives, or calling out racial health disparities—"

"First of all, Finbar, blame narratives and racial health disparities sell newspapers. Our readers don't want to take responsibility for their own maladies; they want to blame something, or someone. Makes everything much, much simpler. Secondly, have you forgotten we've got the Ministry of Equality breathing down our necks right now with this audit. Making the plague racist will earn us some bonus points in our diversity score, you can be sure of that."

Finbar scribbled embarrassed doodles onto his notepad.

"Now that we're all on the same page, I expect all of you staff writers to deliver racialized and politicized plague stories to my desk by five o'clock Friday. Oh, and be sure to give me a plague opinion piece authored by a polyracial pansexual with as many prejudiced pre-existing conditions as possible. We need to hear from more marginalized voices on these matters..."

The Lucid

Leprechaun

Leprechauns were as hard to come by in Fantasmagoria as anywhere, which only partially explained why Finbar was so surprised when he saw one. Even more surprising than the leprechaun was the fact he was about to have his head chopped off. The elusive little green man stood trial on a tree stump in the center of the crowded marketplace for all to see. Standing next to him was a towering guillotine. There were trolls everywhere. The inquisition was on full display.

Finbar wiggled his way to the front of the crowd to get a closer look at the unlucky leprechaun. Under his green stovepipe hat, he wore a roguish smirk. There was a hardly noticeable 'I know something you don't' gleam in his eye. The leprechaun didn't look the least bit worried; he looked mischievous, as you'd expect. Finbar watched as an old troll with a freakishly long nose stepped forward to start the proceedings.

"You stand accused of lucid dreamery," announced the troll.

"You stand accused of cheese dickery," retorted the leprechaun.

Scattered giggles sounded from the crowd. The troll's face darkened with embarrassment.

"As you know, lucid dreaming, defined by law as a dream in which the dreamer is aware they are dreaming, is a serious crime, because it cannot be effectively policed and controlled by the Ministry of Equality. Your dream journals implicate you in lucid dreaming, and—"

The leprechaun interrupted the troll, with a song:

The dream police
They live inside of me head
The dream police
They come to me in me bed
The dream police
They're coming to arrest me
Oh no...

That was too much for the crowd. Finbar laughed long and hard, along with everyone else. The leprechaun was making a mockery of the proceedings. He didn't seem the least bit concerned at the guillotine standing feet from him.

"AS I WAS SAYING!" the troll tried to yell back control of the affair. "Your dream journals were seized. Evidence within those journals indicates you were, eh..." The troll looked uncomfortable. "They indicate you were, well, engaged in a variety of impure acts of umm—"

The leprechaun interrupted him again.

"You mean pogue the hone? Dance the kipples?

Dip the wick? *Fuckery*?"

A muscly troll came forward and punched the wind out of the leprechaun.

"As I was SAYING..." It seemed to Finbar the angrier the troll got, the longer his already long nose grew, as if he were the Pinocchio of rage, instead of lies. "All forms of dreaming, especially lucid dreaming, are criminal. The acts perpetrated within those dreams are also criminal. Inquisitors discovered a wide range of contemptible crimes committed in your dreams. Today, the formal charge being brought against you is for the most heinous crime uncovered—*cultural appropriation.*"

The crowd gasped. Cultural appropriation was a guaranteed death sentence.

"In one of your lucid dreaming episodes, you were found to have commandeered a magic carpet. As if that weren't horrific enough, while in mid-air, your own written records indicate you had a threesome with Shiva, a principal deity of Hinduism, and Muhammed, the revered Islamic prophet. The flying of the magic carpet alone constitutes Muslim cultural appropriation and is punishable by death. The fornication with a Hindu and Abrahamic deity is something so reprehensible we do not have laws in place to penalize it, though I assure you, sir, that it will be prosecuted to the fullest extent. How do you—"

"Objection!" the leprechaun hollered. "Prosecution evidence is demonstrably false. The sexual encounter on the magic carpet was not technically a threesome. It was more a gangbang."

More laughs sounded from the crowd. The stick-nosed troll was not laughing.

"It matters not. How do you answer to these crimes?"

"How *does* one answer a joke?" The leprechaun itched his beard in thought. "A joke is best answered with a joke. Here goes."

The leprechaun cleared his throat, then began.

"Padraic O'Liffy came home drunk every evening toward ten. Now, the missus was never too happy about it, either. So, one night she hides in the cemetery and figures to scare the bejeezus out of him. As poor Pat wanders by, up from behind a tombstone she jumps in a red devil costume, screaming, 'Padraic O'Liffy sure and ya' don't give up your drinkin' and it's to hell I'll take ye.' Pat, undaunted, staggered back and demanded, 'Who the hell ARE you?' To that the missus replied, 'I'm the divil ya' damned old fool,' to which O'Liffy remarked, 'Damned glad to meet you, sir, I'm married to yer sister.'

The crowd erupted in laughter. They were rooting for the leprechaun. The tribunal of course was not. The chief inquisitor's gaping nostrils flared with wolfish ferocity.

"Be that as it may, this holiest of tribunals sentences you to death by beheading for crimes of cultural appropriation consciously committed while unconscious. We shall see how much joking that head of yours does once it is relieved of your heretical body. Do you have any last words?"

"Of course I do." The leprechaun took his hat off, a solemn look on his face.

Once upon a time there was a dildo-nosed troll

Who for a mere shilling sold his precious soul
And bought with it virtue
Of the kind untrue
Living and dying a riled rock without the roll

The leprechaun bowed to the applauding crowd. Finbar clapped, wondering if they'd go forward with the execution. He'd never seen a crowd so in love with the condemned.

A gang of trolls lifted the leprechaun up and laid him down on the guillotine. The leprechaun didn't resist. There was no point. The trolls easily held the tiny trickster in place, baring the flesh of his neck. A masked troll tugged down on the rope that raised the bright, angled blade of the death machine. When the troll let the rope loose, the weighted blade dropped so swiftly Finbar hardly saw it fall. It sliced cleanly through the leprechaun's neck, sending the little redhead rolling through the crowd like a soccer ball, spectators fending it away with their feet.

The crowd stood in silent horror, but only for a moment, because the leprechaun was only dead for a moment. Finbar watched in amazement as the leprechaun's headless body rose from the guillotine by some magic, or trickery. The trolls were panic-stricken at the sight, scattering this way and that in frightened disbelief. The long-nosed chief inquisitor looked to have had a heart attack, first clutching at his chest, then falling from the platform. He did not get up.

The crowd watched in silent incredulity as the headless leprechaun skipped down from the guillotine. He made his way through the stunned crowd and found his severed head. He picked it up and skipped back to the guillotine platform with it. Holding his own head up by the hair, he turned it so it faced the crowd. The eyes opened, then the mouth, singing a song:

> *Chase me Charlie, find me barley*
> *Up the leg of me drawers,*
> *If you don't believe me, come and feel me,*
> *Up the leg of me drawers.*

The leprechaun fastened his head back onto his body and proceeded to dance a jig. The crowd went wild. He jigged in circles around the useless guillotine. He reeled in mockery of the government, and of trolls. He tapped his buckled shoes, and they struck the platform like long overdue thunder. Everyone cheered and clapped in time with the dance, and it was like the inquisition never was. Finbar marveled at the spectacular scene.

It was the happiest execution in history.

The Old Man

and the Wind

Finbar was on his way home from work one blustery day when he passed the beautiful, blonde brick bungalow where the odd old bachelor, who emerged only in the company of the wind, lived. Finbar saw him swaying on the porch swing with his eyes shut, as usual. Aristotle said he was a seaman, and he looked it. He wore a long, navy blue sailor's pea coat and dark corduroy pants. Strands of gray hair poked through the holes of a raggedy peaked cap. A corncob pipe protruded through his white whiskers.

Finbar approached, packet of sea salt in hand. He rubbed some of the crystals between his fingers and held them over the old man's sleepy smile, just under the nostrils. It worked. The old man opened his eyes and leapt from the swing in surprise. Finbar took the opportunity to kindly introduce himself and finally ask the old man why he was so in love with the wind.

The old man said it wasn't the wind he was in love with. It was a mermaid.

-

When the old man was a young man, he'd been a lighthouse keeper. He operated a stubby stone lighthouse on an even stubbier speck of rubble peeking from an endless sea at the edge of the known world. The lighthouse was so far removed from civilization, he often went weeks without seeing a single ship. Much of the time, the fish were his only company. So, he fished.

Late one afternoon, he dangled his legs from the skinny lighthouse pier, fishing line in the water, waiting patiently for dinner to bite. He wouldn't have to wait long. It was prime fishing season—that time of the year when the winds blew toward the lighthouse pier, bringing forth all flavors of delectable fish from the ocean depths. A curiously strong wind blew that day, as if making up for lost time. There was a hint of something clammy in those squalls.

The lighthouse keeper was rebaiting his hook when out of the corner of his eye he saw something flapping in the water close to the shore behind him. He saw hands flailing through the white caps and a long-haired head occasionally bobbing out of the water. The man couldn't believe his eyes. Then it screamed for help, and he couldn't believe his ears. It looked like a girl, drowning! He dove into the water and dragged her to shore. There, he saw to his amazement that it was no ordinary girl at all. It was a mermaid.

She looked like the Starbuck's mermaid, with this endless, pumpkin orange hair woven through a silver circlet. Her skin was pale as it comes, almost translucent. The jade and silver of her tail glittered like jeweled seaweed in the remnants of daylight. She had one of those legendary faces worth launching a thousand ships. Her lips were amethyst. Her sapphire eyes twinkled with wonder. The lighthouse keeper's eyes twinkled with something more than wonder, because by that point he was already well in love.

He asked the mermaid what was wrong, hoping whatever was wrong would stay that way. Broken tailfin? Bad gills? Perhaps a sea monster in the vicinity? No, no, no. It was much simpler than that. She sadly told him that she couldn't swim. Not a single stroke. She said she was probably the only mermaid in the world who couldn't swim. She said she was a misfit.

The lighthouse keeper said there were no misfits on his island, only guests, and he'd be honored if she'd be his. She said yes, as though she had a choice. He built a home for her in the shallow lighthouse harbor. The mermaid was sad at not being able to swim, but pleased to be safe in the harbor. Of course, the man was happy to have her there. She was more than a mere cure for lighthouse loneliness. To him, she was the most magnificent creature in all the seven seas. He would sit up in his lighthouse and stare down at her.

Instead of shining the lighthouse light out to sea to help ships navigate the rough waters, he would shine it down on her. Untold numbers of ships were lost or sank as a result of the distracted lighthouse keeper.

The mermaid and the man often dined together out on the edge of the pier. Sometimes, the sea would mirror the stars so perfectly, the horizon line on the water would disappear, leaving the two all alone in the center of their own private galaxy. He would tell her stories of life on land, of werewolves and wolpertingers. She would tell him stories of the world underneath it, of serpents and Scylla. He sang her sea shanties of shipboard tasks, of hauling anchor and heaving the capstan. She sang him sea shanties of enchanted waters, of sirens singing and hydras howling. They talked and talked, stopping only to kiss.

One day, the mermaid told the man she must learn to swim before the seasons changed. When the winds blew back out to sea taking her with them, she would be drowned. She asked the man if he would teach her to swim. He agreed, happy to save her, though anxious at the thought of her leaving. He spent his days practicing with her in the harbor, first acclimating her to the waves, then teaching her fundamental movements and strokes.

It wasn't long before the mermaid was swimming like, well, a mermaid. Some days, she would venture far off into the sea, all alone. The lighthouse keeper worried for her when she left, but the winds always carried her back safely. By the time the seasons changed and the winds shifted out to sea, the mermaid was a masterful swimmer and well prepared to leave. Before setting off, she promised the lighthouse keeper she would return to him when the seasons changed and the prevailing winds returned to the lighthouse. The lighthouse keeper was miserable at her leaving, but hopeful for her return.

At every turn of the season, the lighthouse keeper kept a vigilant watch over the sea, into the face of the changed winds. The mermaid honored her promise, returning to the lighthouse in the arms of those winds, if only for a little while. The lighthouse keeper was happiest when she returned. They swam in the harbor, dined on the pier above and below the stars, told stories and sang songs the way they used to. The mermaid returned year after year, and the lighthouse keeper looked forward to little else on his lonely island.

Time passed, years turned to decades, and the young lighthouse keeper changed. The moonlight dyed his hair silver. The sunlight colored his skin bronze. The salty ocean air wrinkled his face. A lifetime of thoughts wrinkled his mind. He'd grown old. Eventually, he could no longer walk up the lighthouse stairs to perform his navigational duties. Knowing he would soon be relieved, he asked the mermaid to take him away with her into the sea, down to the hidden ocean depths, wherever it is mermaids go. She refused, explaining that she couldn't possibly drown the one who had rescued her from drowning. Instead, she cast a merciful spell on the old lighthouse keeper. Whenever the winds blew in from the great sea and touched him, he would feel as though he were underwater, with her.

In the wind, he would join her again in the sea.

-

So, the old man sat on his front porch only when

the winds rose, submerged by the mermaid's spell. He closed his eyes and found himself on the sea floor. He saw herds of sunken spirits galloping with the undercurrent. He saw Capricorn goats, sea horses, and selkies all charging along the sea bed. Every sort of sea creature swam by him, all around him, even straight through him. He saw his mermaid, swam with her, and kissed her once again. Those briny kisses were of the magical sort. They turned the water iridescent, like splatters of every color paint on a shapeless canvas. Each new kiss brought forth a new burst of watercolors, and he was the happiest fish in the sea, on his front porch.

The End of Time

One lazy Sunday, Finbar feasted on a late breakfast at the Tipsy Timepiece Tavern. There were only a handful of customers at the tavern that morning. Finbar was the only one sitting at the bar. He ate his Tabasco-drenched eggs, drank his Tabasco-drenched bloody mary, and passed the time with the time working behind the bar. He and the grandfather clock were engaged in a deeply philosophical pub talk regarding the nature of time, memory, and taverns. Finbar believed the purpose of taverns and alcohol was to forget. Aristotle believed the opposite to be true.

"People come to the Tipsy Timepiece to forget,"

Finbar reasoned. "The past isn't doing anyone any favors. Everyone says growing up is the hard part, but I don't think so. I think it's the growing down that's hardest. And it's not the getting old, it's the realization we were once young. It's the remembering that makes it so difficult. I was happiest as a kid, before I hardly had a past to remember, before the unsorted baggage of years crowded my skull. I come to the Tipsy Timepiece to forget the past, to be that same careless kid." Finbar took a whiff of his drink. "This here drink smells timeless, with a hint of tomato."

"No it doesn't. That drink smells of a story," Aristotle countered. "Taverns are storytelling institutions. Stories, even the made-up sort, they're born from memory. You can't have stories without memories. Well, no good ones at least. Take the story of Fantasmagoria. Yeah, it might be sad in parts with the inquisition and all, but you can't have happily ever after from start to finish. That would make for the worst story of all time. Remembering is not the problem. Forgetting is. Forget the past and you forget yourself..."

Without warning, the tavern front door burst open
with such force that it flew off the hinges and into the
bar, crushing an unlucky gnome sitting at a nearby
table for two. A mob of angry trolls charged in, filling
every inch of the bar. They swarmed the old
grandfather clock, dragging him from behind the bar
to the middle of the dance floor. Finbar hardly had a
chance to get off his barstool in the time it took the
trolls to raid the place. When he did stand up, he was
instantly encircled and restrained by no less than four
trolls, one for each limb, with hands like manacles of
cold, bony steel.

Finbar watched as an elderly, important-looking
troll marched slowly through the broken-down door.
Finbar recognized him. He was one of those dreaded
chief inquisitors, responsible for the interrogation and
sentencing of heretics. The chief inquisitor sauntered
to the dance floor, first circling and examining, then
standing in front of Aristotle. The bar quieted. Finbar
could hear the ticking on the grandfather clock's face.

"I presume you are the one and only Aristotle,
proprietor of this establishment?"

"Let me go, you chicken-livered skinflint!" Aristotle struggled hopelessly.

"I'll take that as a yes." The old troll smiled hatefully. "Being a grandfather clock, you identify as *time*? Would that be correct?"

"Of course I do! Have you ever met a clock who wasn't time?"

"Certainly not." The troll turned to address the bar.

"Time has been declared illegal. Why? The Ministry of Equality has designated time as discriminatory, because time is not equally distributed among all citizens of Fantasmagoria. The young have more time than the old. The healthy have more time than the sick. Elves have more time than ogres. The properties of time are clearly unfair, and in direct conflict with the government's goal of an absolutely equal society."

The troll turned back around, standing face-to-face with Aristotle.

"In accordance with the new law, all clocks have been canceled. The tracking of time is illegal. The ticking of clocks, such as your own, will no longer be tolerated."

The grandfather clock hocked a tremendous loogie into the chief inquisitor's face. A troll rushed from the bar with a towel, cleaning it off. At the same time, a muscly ogre ducked through the door. He joined the chief inquisitor on the dance floor with a boulder-smashing sledgehammer.

"Aristotle, owner of the Tipsy Timepiece Tavern, I sentence you to death by sledgehammering for the possession of time and discrimination of the sick, elderly, and mortal. Any last words?"

The old clock took a deep breath as he seemed to relax and accept his fate.

"Lost time is never found. All you mad trolls, this senseless inquisition, the never-ending quest for virtue, it has already lost Fantasmagoria more time than the ticking of a trillion clocks. There is only so much time. Keep killing it, and without a doubt you'll kill yourself along with it."

The ogre handed the chief inquisitor the sledgehammer, or tried to. The old troll couldn't lift it an inch off the ground. It was far too heavy. He tried for a few awkward minutes before ordering the ogre to do the job for him. The ogre stepped forward, easily picking up the sledgehammer. The dance floor cleared to make room for the grim execution.

Finbar couldn't believe what was about to happen. He struggled to move, to save his friend, but there was no point. The trolls tightened their grip on him. Aristotle didn't try to run. He stood expressionless and still, apart from the slow tick of the second hand on his clock-face.

The ogre backed away, then rushed forward, sledgehammer raised. He swung it mightily, and it struck like the hammer of Thor, atomizing the clock's head with an eerie, glass-shattering thud. A thousand tiny bits of spring, metal, wood, and other clock guts went flying in all directions. The sledgehammer made a gaping hole in the brick wall behind where Aristotle stood headless, before collapsing onto the dance floor.

"NOOOOOOOOOOOOOO!!!" Finbar screamed.

The chief inquisitor looked at Finbar, then down on the broken clock. "Your *time* is up." He spat onto the remains. "As for the rest of you, we will be confiscating all watches and other timekeeping devices. This establishment is closed until further notice. Good day!"

The trolls confiscated watches from the few traumatized patrons in the tavern, including Finbar's favorite pocket watch. There were a few odd clocks taken down from the walls. An hourglass was shattered on the dance floor next to Aristotle. The jukebox was even smashed to bits, because it measured the time of songs. When the trolls were finished, there was no evidence of time ever having been in the tavern.

Finbar sat at the bar crying for his friend, for all the lost time.

A Genuine

Offense

Finbar was walking to work one windless morning when he was surprised by the sight of the old man. It was the first time Finbar had ever seen the man outside without a noticeable breeze. He was packing a wagon. It looked as though he were moving away. Finbar asked him whatever was he doing out and about without the wind.

"You didn't hear? The government canceled the wind."

"How, and why, does one cancel the wind?"

"Geographic Privilege Act. The act was passed because citizens of certain inclement geographies were found to be inherently disadvantaged due to poor weather. As it turns out, fair weather is not fairly distributed across Fantasmagoria. The west is generally warmer than the east. The south receives much more sunlight than the north. The midwest is less humid than the southwest. And on and on. The government intends to more equitably distribute the weather. One of the first steps they took was to normalize wind speeds across all regions. For that purpose, a new climate-controlling technology was implemented, which reduced all wind speeds to a consistent, but hardly noticeable six miles per hour. In that way, the wind was effectively canceled."

"I'm so sorry..."

It seemed to Finbar when the wind ceased breathing, so might the old man. Without the wind, the mermaid's spell was broken. He would probably never see her again.

"Don't be sorry. I'm headed back out to sea! I shall

set sail somewhere the wind still whistles wild and wonderfully, somewhere without laws to govern what was never meant to be governed. Somewhere free, the way it used to be. With any luck, I'll find me a mermaid. *The* mermaid."

"Well, good luck to you. I hope you find her again."

"Thanks, laddie. No doubt I'll need a dash of luck to get where I'm going. I'm no longer afraid of squalls, storms, or sea monsters. I'm afraid of their cancellation. Farewell…"

With a wink the old man was gone, never to be seen in the kingdom again.

-

That day at the office started uneventfully. Which of course makes perfect sense, because all of life's great catastrophes blindside you on some otherwise uneventful weekday. They tend to be things that would never have otherwise ever crossed your mind. Such was the case with Finbar.

He was at work, not working. Having just finished his censorship duties for the day, he sat at his desk reading *Meditations*, by Marcus Aurelius—an illegal masterpiece of stoic philosophy. Finbar wasn't worried about reading illegal books in the privacy of his own cubicle. Banned books were surging in popularity. Anyone who was anyone was reading banned books. Sinning was wildly popular in that regard.

Finbar looked up from the book and saw a lone troll standing in the distance. It was unusual to see a troll in his part of the office, and all alone at that. Trolls are pack animals. The troll was talking to the office secretary, his back turned to Finbar. Finbar watched as the troll lifted his head and turned slowly around, as if he was aware of Finbar. The troll stared at him awhile unmoving, head tilting in a curious sort of way. Finbar stared back at the troll's face. It was a surreal, disarranged thing. The more Finbar stared at him, the more the troll's features changed. One second he had the head of skeleton, next a gorgon, then three gorgons, then a massive sphinx head. He laughed a laugh so deep it sounded like it came from the basement mailroom. The dark shape of him convulsed as he approached Finbar. He laughed that deep laugh, growing louder and louder the closer he came, until he was standing right next to Finbar.

Finbar didn't run. He didn't argue. In fact, he didn't say anything at all. He knew he was under arrest. There was no need to make a scene. He put the book down and stood up, his worst fears realized. As he followed the troll out of the office, he felt as though he were on fire, hooves to horns. The soles of his feet sizzled with every step, as though the carpet burned below him. His arms dangled like noodles from his side, barely working. His body refused to sweat, to cool him. His shoulders felt liked overheated rotors. His head was dizzy, begging for shade from the fluorescent lights, begging for him to hide, or run. He couldn't have run if he wanted to. He could hardly walk. He hobbled hopelessly after the troll, his back bent like an old man.

The troll led him out of the office and into the back of a wagon that was waiting outside. The wagon was filled with other newly arrested criminals. There was a hobgoblin, a handful of dwarves, an ogre in a straightjacket, and plenty of bruised and beaten elves. It was a wretched scene. Finbar sat on the bench next to the hobgoblin, putting his head down, horns in his hands.

"Whatcha in for?" the hobgoblin asked him.

Finbar wondered what he was in for. The reading of banned books? The practicing of stoicism? Had he used an illegal word in a letter one hundred years ago? Unconscious racism? Cultural appropriation? Lucid dreaming? Acts of cultural appropriation while lucid dreaming?

As it turned out, it was none of those things.

He was arrested for being himself.

-

Although Finbar had been arrested for being himself, he felt nothing like himself as he sat chained to the wall of his dungeon. Finbar was a faun. Fauns are half human-half goat. Finbar had always considered himself a civilized specimen, much more human than goat. But in that cage, he was all goat, and treated like one. He was fed garbage. He pissed and shat in the corner. He slept on a bed of damp, rotten hay. A goatish stench filled every corner of his cell. He felt like a filthy, funky, domesticated nothing.

Finbar sat in the despondent darkness of the dungeon with nothing to do but wait for his lawyer. He was surprised to have even been assigned a lawyer. Most inquisition cases were tried without one. Generally, only the most important defendants were granted a lawyer. Finbar didn't consider himself a heretic of any importance. He would have been surprised if more than a handful of spectators showed up for his trial and execution thereafter.

Finbar heard the echo of heavy footsteps coming down the dungeon stairs and through the passage toward his cell. He hadn't seen light in so long that when the hallway filled with it, he thought he was dreaming. Whatever he was expecting of a lawyer, it certainly wasn't what came. A wizened old man in a mossy robe peered through the steel bars, his face glowing golden in the light from the candelabra he carried. His eyes shone wide and bright under big bushy eyebrows and a weathered, pointed hat. He didn't look like a lawyer. He looked like a wizard.

"That's because I *am* a wizard," said the wizard, reading Finbar's mind. "It's hotter than a whorehouse on nickel night down here. Water?"

The wizard handed Finbar a flagon of water. Finbar drank every last drop. In a dungeon, there was no telling when or how much water you will receive.

"My name is Woodrow the Wizard. I'll be representing you in your upcoming trial."

The wizard sat down on a haystack next to Finbar, lighting a long pipe with one of his candles.

"Who appointed you?" Finbar asked.

"I appointed myself. You see, we have a mutual friend at the *Elven Standard*. That bug-eyed dwarf Ivan? Your boss? He and I go back to roughly the dawn of time. I owe him a favor. Many favors, actually. Because of that, my services in this case are offered without charge. Speaking of charges, do you know what you are charged with?"

"No."

"I didn't think so. You're charged with the crime of being yourself."

The wizard sent smoke rings of all shapes, sizes, and colors wafting throughout the dungeon. Finbar was thankful for the smoky fragrance, which was effective in lessening the goat-stench.

"Since when is it a crime to be yourself?"

"Technically, it has only been a crime since you were arrested, though the inquisition has been arresting citizens for as much and calling it by a variety of other names for some time now. With the exception of elves, I've never seen anyone placed under arrest on such a narrow charge of individuality. It could be that fauns as a class of citizen have recently been made illegal, but I doubt it. I haven't heard of any other fauns being arrested. You seem to have been targeted by the inquisition. Do you have any idea why?"

"Couldn't say for sure, no..."

It could have been any number of things, but Finbar had a sneaking suspicion it had to do with the Tipsy Timepiece Tavern. He guessed that his own arrest and the execution of Aristotle were tied to that fateful day when the troll inquisitor had been heaved out of the tavern front window.

"Well, it doesn't matter. In most of these cases, the tribunal is conjuring up fabricated evidence anyway. Tell me though, what do you identify as? Just a plain old faun? Are you queer, trans, or anything remotely high on the Ministry's hierarchy of oppression?"

"Nope. Just a run-of-the-mill faun."

"That's a shame. A transfeminine, two-spirited cyclops burned down an orphanage last month and got off with community service. The slap on the wrist was mostly on account of the arsonist being a transfeminine, two-spirited cyclops. If you were a marginalized citizen, we would have a much greater chance of leniency from the tribunal."

"Jeez, sorry..." Finbar said, wishing he was at least bisexual.

"Don't be sorry for who you are. That's what we're defending against. You have every right to be yourself. Tell me though, how are you feeling? Are you prepared for the trial?"

"When is the trial?"

"You didn't know? The trial is this afternoon."

The Trial

A troll shoved Finbar forth from the dungeon with his legs shackled and hands bound tightly behind his back. He had been in the cell for several days, so was relieved to be outside again, though it was a dreary afternoon. The sky was perfectly suited for a funeral. The sun was hidden behind smoky plumes of ash. A steady rain fell straight down as it always did in those days. There was no wind to blow it any other way. The wind was canceled.

Finbar wondered if he would also be canceled.

He was seated in the back of a rickety, horse-drawn carriage. It bumped and slogged unsteadily through the muddy streets toward the marketplace, where the trial and likely execution were to take place. Arriving after a short but uncomfortable ride, Finbar emerged from the carriage to find the area mostly empty of people, except for a handful of trolls readying the rituals. It would have been unusual for it to be full of people. Spectators normally came only for the execution.

Finbar was helped out of the carriage by his wizard counsel who had been waiting for him. He was pleased to find the rain had weakened to a drizzle. The wizard led him to a chair behind a small desk where the two were seated. Across the marketplace, they were faced with another desk where the tribunal prosecutor sat. He was a younger-looking troll dressed in an expensive-looking suit. The trial was presided over by an elderly, white-robed chief inquisitor who sat on a raised bench between the them.

An ominous grumble of thunder announced the start of the trial. The chief inquisitor began.

"Finbar Finnegan, you stand before this holiest of tribunals faced with the grave charge of being yourself, a first-degree form of individualism. The penalty for such a crime is death by burning." Finbar noticed the tree-like stake that had been erected for that very purpose. "I will hear brief arguments from the prosecution and your own defense before rendering a verdict. Prosecutor, you may begin."

The prosecutor emerged from behind his desk, marching slowly toward Finbar and the wizard as he began what was clearly a well-rehearsed speech.

"In general, individualist cultures tend to conceive of people as self-directed and autonomous, and they tend to prioritize independence and uniqueness as cultural values. Collectivist cultures such as Fantasmagoria, on the other hand, tend to see people as connected with others and embedded in a broader social context—as such, they tend to emphasize interdependence, intersectionality, and social conformity. Individualist cultures and ideologies are, of course, highly illegal, because they result in a wide-range of inequalities and unfairness."

The troll turned, marching now slowly toward the chief inquisitor as he continued.

"The defendant has exhibited deviant, individualistic tendencies throughout his entire life. He is unique, self-reliant, independent, and free-thinking. His uniqueness is evidenced by his artistic interests and bohemian lifestyle, which have a tendency toward self-creation and experimentation as opposed to tradition and conformity. Does the defense deny these sinful tendencies?"

The wizard patted Finbar on the hand in assurance before stepping forward from behind the desk. A handful of spectators gathered on the outskirts to watch the proceedings.

"We do not deny these tendencies. Fauns, as a species, are simply more individualistic. The Ministry of Equality claims everyone is born equally capable, competent, and in nearly every other way the same. This is simply not true. Creatures of Fantasmagoria are not born equally beautiful, strong, sensible, or anything else for that matter. They are born as their own distinctive selves. The crime in this case is no crime it all. It is the way of the world."

The prosecutor paused in surprised

contemplation. He expected a defense of the defendant, not this audacious questioning of government ideology, which was highly illegal. Finbar nervously tapped his hooves below the desk, wondering whether the wizard's strategy might work, waiting for the prosecutor's response.

"Sir wizard, surely you do not mean to claim to me, and to this holy tribunal, that there exists a meaningful, innate biological difference between the citizens of Fantasmagoria?"

"I mean to claim just that. There are inherent differences between each and every citizen of this vast kingdom. Mermaids are better swimmers than goblins. Goblins are better miners than mermaids. Leprechauns tend to have far higher rates of alcoholism than pretty much everyone. Vampires tend to outlive elves. Elves do, on average, have slightly higher IQs than ogres. The reason? IQ is heritable. Just like a tail fin. Just like everything else."

The wizard turned away from the prosecutor, now speaking directly to the chief inquisitor.

"There is nothing wrong with these differences. It

is not a sin or crime to be born this way or that. Who we are as individuals is not something that must be forcefully corrected by religion, or by the government. Each of the kingdom's creatures has the right to be themselves, and to be proud of who they are, just as this faun sitting here does."

"Your argument insinuates then that stereotypes are true?" the prosecutor was almost laughing as he asked the question. Stereotyping was punishable by flaying.

"Some stereotypes are, of course, false, but yes some are inconvenient truths. That of course does not mean individuals ought to be treated unfairly, or discriminated against. It does not mean that certain groups or races should be viewed as inferior, or superior to others. It simply means we are all different. Our differences have made Fantasmagoria the cultural mecca it is today. The mitigation of these differences is hurting us. The fact that we citizens are all being forced in the name of equality to assimilate into a culture of oneness and wokeness is a grave mistake. If we are to be a free society, we must be free to be ourselves, acknowledging and respecting each of us for what we truly are – different."

Finbar looked on in astonishment. The rogue wizard was making a mockery of the tribunal, inquisition, and of widely accepted church doctrine in front of the enforcing religious agency itself. Even crazier, it seemed to be working. The prosecutor fumbled clumsily at the papers behind his desk. The chief inquisitor watched in annoyance, waiting for the prosecutor to act. It took him several minutes of fumbling before he finally emerged from behind his desk, holding forth a scrap of evidence.

"Oppression!" the prosecutor announced with gusto. Here was his gotcha moment. Finbar stared sickly at the paper, wondering what it might be.

"How would the defendant answer to the oppressive history of his ancestors? Here in my hand I have the defendant's family tree. This document contains evidence that one of the defendant's ancestors was complicit in the wholesale slaughter of indigenous peoples. History cannot be denied!"

"History cannot be denied, though it can be

forgiven," the wizard calmly explained. "Finbar is no more guilty of the past than the rest of this kingdom. Name me a race that hasn't committed an atrocity against another? Elves kill dwarves. Dwarves kill goblins. Goblins kill humans. Humans kill humans, and everything else. You trolls are guilty of these very crimes as we speak. This inquisition is a deliberate genocide of innocent, free-thinking citizens like Finbar Finnegan. There was never a more dangerous time to reject accepted opinions, especially those concerning the Ministry of Equality and its divisive dogma."

"What of the Ministry of Equality and its divisive dogma?" the chief inquisitor intervened for the first time. "What of the mission for equality in Fantasmagoria? Is that not a noble cause?"

"Noble, yes. Realistic, no. Could an orc ever hope to have the same foresight as an oracle? Will a gremlin ever have the same industrial job prospects as a gogmagog? Could a troll ever hope to match a titan in battle? No, no, no. In a world where we're all different, absolute equality of opportunity is an impossible dream. Equality of outcome is dystopian nightmare."

"Then tell me, oh wise wizard, why am I employed if the war for equality and social justice is without hope? Why any of this inquisition in the first place?"

"Good question." The wizard stroked his beard in thought. "I think you, these trolls, this tribunal, and this entire inquisition are an overcorrection in the once needed fight for equality, civil rights, and social justice. That fight was fought by ancestors far braver than you, and it has already been, for the most part, won. Widespread, structural oppression in the modern age is a myth. Slavery has been outlawed for over five generations. All citizens have the right to vote. State segregation is a thing of the past. It is illegal to pay elves more than dwarves, goblins, fairies, or any other race, for the same job. All citizens have a right to public and government services. It seems all we don't have a right to is a fair trial!"

The chief inquisitor stood up, gesturing excitedly with his gangly arms as he spoke.

"If the war for equality is won, how do you explain the persisting wealth gap? How do you explain the underrepresentation of imps at top colleges and overrepresentation in the prison population? Surely these are evidences for widespread discrimination and racism?"

"Accept our differences as citizens, and you can accept the fact there will *always* be differences in proportions of wealth, criminal activity, and educational attainment. Because you believe in inherent equality, essentially from birth, it reasons you would attribute any and all racial disparities to structural discrimination. You are wrong in that attribution, but you already know that. Don't you?"

The prosecutor, chief-inquisitor, and the rest of the troll tribunal stared at the wizard in stunned silence. Finbar was horrified. There could be no good ending for him after such a heretical tirade. And the wizard wasn't even finished...

"I wonder who among you trolls would *ever* admit to progress or victory in the fight for equality? I think none. If you did, you would all suddenly find yourselves out of the job, as would thousands of professor-priests, chief creature officers, diversity auditors, social scientists, social justice warriors, executioners, and chief-inquisitors. You *need* the inquisition. In truth, you're the *only* ones who need the inquisition."

The wizard stood in the center of the marketplace, glaring at the chief inquisitor. The chief inquisitor stood staring fiercely back. Finbar watched, seeing for the first time a strange resemblance between the two elders. He could sense the strain between them, drawn from eye to eye, each reading the other's mind in speechless debate. After a long, awkward staring contest, it was the troll who withdrew his gaze.

The crowd of spectators was growing larger. Finbar recognized a few friends from the neighborhood and newspaper. All of them were listening intently. It was unclear to them who was on trial – the faun, or the inquisition itself. The wizard turned and spoke to them.

"The inquisition seeks not to heal Fantasmagoria, but to divide it. The stock-in-trade of this tribunal is moral outrage and collective madness. These troll inquisitors are a salaried class of liars and lunatics. They are profiteers of panic. It is no wonder the River of Deceit flows high and swift as ever. The headwaters of lies and madness originating from this corrupt kingdom are never-ending!"

The growing crowd cheered in defiance of the tribunal. A faint glimmer of hope rose within Finbar's heart. There was a chance the crowd might rise in rebellion. There was a chance he was witnessing the beginning of the end of the inquisition. There was a chance he'd survive.

"You have not heard?" the chief inquisitor interrupted the cheering, a villainous smirk on his face. "The River of Deceit has been renamed the River of Virtue. It flows high and fast not with lies and madness, but with righteousness and retribution. The river would be perfectly suited to drown a certain dissident wizard. It is said that only the faithful float in the River of Virtue. Perhaps we should test your own buoyancy?"

"Perhaps you should try, your holiness."

At a signal from the chief inquisitor, a gang of trolls bum-rushed the wizard. Just before they reached him, something unusual happened. The whole of the marketplace darkened so quickly and thoroughly, it was as though someone had magically flicked off the lights. Street lanterns blew out, the sky turned black, all the surrounding shop windows darkened. Finbar sat in confused oblivion for only a few seconds, before a great, glowing sword appeared where the wizard had been. It danced through the darkness, cleaving the dumbfounded trolls with savage proficiency. The marketplace devolved into a temporary chaos of croaking, howling, and cursing troll sounds. The wizard butchered half the tribunal in what seemed like no more than a few seconds.

It was, of course, an elemental spell of darkness from the wizard that had without warning turned the lights off. When they turned back on, a dozen or more trolls lay slain in the center of the marketplace, now a welling pool of blood. The prosecutor sat behind his desk, headless. Finbar sat behind his desk, an oh-shit look on his face. The chief inquisitor wore a similar look of oh-shitness as he stared down from his bench, taking in the murderous scene. The wizard was nowhere to be seen.

The crowd remained where they had stood before the wizard's spell turned off the lights. They all looked up to the chief inquisitor, who regained his composure after realizing he was still alive and the wizard was gone. He stood up, banging his gavel on the sounding block wildly. He found Finbar with his greasy eyes, pointing the gavel at him in blame.

"Guilty! Guilty! Guilty! This holiest of tribunals sentences you to death by BURNING!"

Death by Fire

There Finbar was, tied firmly to a stake in the middle of the marketplace, in the middle of his worst nightmare come true. The few trolls left unharmed by the wizard were at work piling firewood and kindling below the little platform on which he stood. In typical inquisition fashion, the crowd of spectators had grown as the moment of execution neared. The night had arrived as well. Stars blinked to life like faraway witnesses from the moonless sky above.

Finbar was not all that nervous considering he was about to be slowly roasted alive. He had, for the most part, come to terms with his fate before the trial even started, starved of hope and humanity in his dungeon. There was no point in brooding, or even thinking. He looked up to the sublime sky instead of down at the madness of the inquisition. It *was* a perfect night, and he had quite the view of it standing there, high above the crowd. The sky had cleared of the earlier storm clouds. A barely visible layer of velvet frosted the far horizon, reminding Finbar it wasn't that long ago his last sun had set. The stars were worth gazing at that night. It seemed to Finbar he had hardly noticed them before, and for that he felt as if his whole short life had been a shame. He wished he had looked up at the stars more often, when he'd had the chance.

Finbar looked down from the sky to check on the progress of his execution. Timber was stacked high. Tinder was strategically placed. Dead trolls were cleared from the scene. Living trolls were standing at attention. The crowd was still and silent, necks craning for a better view.

All was ready.

The chief inquisitor climbed onto his lectern, reading the sentence aloud for all to hear. Finbar watched his mouth move, but chose not to listen to the words. There was no point. He knew the charges, and the sentence. When the chief inquisitor had finished, a diminutive troll marched forth. The troll brandished a torch, the flames of which would be the source of the blaze that would soon engulf Finbar. He watched as the curious torch flame danced dangerously toward him. He felt like he was watching someone else's execution, like he was just one of the crowd. It all seemed too strange to be happening, when something even stranger happened.

The torch blew out. *In the wind.*

A torch blowing out in the wind may not, on the surface, appear strange, but it was in fact more than strange. The Geographic Privilege Act had effectively canceled high winds. The winds were centrally administered and controlled by the government. The winds shouldn't have been blowing anywhere near hard enough to blow out a match, let alone a torch. Yet, they *were* blowing. They blew harder and harder.

Finbar felt the wind on his face and smiled. It was a sorely missed breath of fresh, forgotten air. He squinted off into the distance toward the source of the wind. There, he noticed what at first he guessed to be two newly appeared stars behaving unnaturally. The stars twirled and blinked erratically in the darkness, like a pair of faraway fireflies. Then they grew larger and climbed higher, as if they were the headlights of some soaring ghost train.

The sudden, unexpected change in weather stopped the execution ritual entirely. Everyone in the marketplace, trolls and spectators alike, stared in silent astonishment at the mysterious, now fast-approaching lights. The wind strengthened as the glowing orbs drew near. The crowd watched until the lights were upon them, until it became clear what it was they were. And when they discerned the simmering source, their curiosity turned to dread.

The two lights were the smoldering eyes of a vast, golden-garnet dragon.

The dragon was without question the largest and most menacing configuration of matter Finbar had ever laid eyes on. He judged the head alone to be larger than his apartment building. The body was the length of a city block or more. The claws looked like oversized bulldozer blades. Its wing span was immeasurable. One single flap blew away half the marketplace crowd like tiny shreds of paper. Finbar was lucky to be tied to the stake, or he too would have blown away.

The remnants of the crowd watched in horror as the dragon swooped down, hovering low over the chief inquisitor, who stood there with a look of stupefied terror on his face. The dragon inhaled with such force, he seemed to suck all the oxygen from the marketplace. Finbar and everyone else struggled to catch their breath, watching as the dragon vomited a stream of white hot flame, scorching the chief inquisitor so thoroughly that when the smoke cleared, the troll skeleton remained where it stood on the now incinerated bench.

The crowd fled in a frenzy. Finbar, of course, couldn't go anywhere. He remained tied to the stake, watching helplessly as the dragon wreaked havoc. After the marketplace, it soared higher over the city, occasionally hurtling down, burning indiscriminately, turning roads into rivers of flame and buildings into bonfires. In just a few minutes, the city was burning hot as Rome under the torches of Nero. Clever sparks leapt nimbly from roof to roof, carried through the air in the arms of the outlawed wind. Whole neighborhoods of row houses burned brightly into the night before crumbling to the ground. Fires crackled and roared over the shrieks and wails of the helpless citizens. Fantasmagoria was an unquenchable conflagration.

The city itself was without defenses. There were no hails of arrows, dragon-slaying knights, or black mages to bring the dragon down. There were no warriors at all. Dragon-battling warriors had been repurposed as social justice warriors. The military had been canceled. The dragon defense budget had been reallocated to the defense of marginalized classes. Finbar was surprised it had taken a dragon so long to realize the city was so completely helpless.

The dragon eventually made his way to the capital building, seat of the central government—the Ministry of Equality. That building likely drew the dragon's attention because it was situated on a hilltop at the center of town. It was an appetizing, wedding-cake style cast-iron dome rising hundreds of feet into the air. The dragon stooped over it, examining it a while, unsure whether to eat it or burn it. Finbar saw the silhouette of a little troll in one of the upper story windows. It was likely some governmental scholar studying culturally sensitive pronouns and racial categorizations for the very same dragon that was incinerating the entire kingdom. Finbar wondered what politically correct phrase the government would concoct for a civilization-ending dragon. Proboscised airborne reptilian? Warm-blooded vertebrate? Certainly, a gender-neutral pronoun would be in order. They. Them. Theirs. Offending a dragon is risky.

Not that any of that mattered now. Nothing mattered now. The dragon had reduced the capital building to a pile of ashes with little effort. Finbar saw it burn, and the dreadful irony in it burning how it did. The Ministry of Equality was gone. Fantasmagoria was no more.

-

Finbar watched the world burn from his own

burning at the stake. He was, of course, only able to watch the world burn because he himself had yet to be burned. But that would soon change. The tinder below him had just been brought to life by some stray spark. The fire spread quickly in the ceaseless wind. As it turned out, Finbar would be burnt at the stake after all. Only this time, there would be no theatrical production. There would be no one left to even notice.

The flames were singeing the hair on Finbar's hooves when the wizard reappeared, dashing through the burning marketplace on a smoke-stained stallion. He untied Finbar from the stake with not a second left to spare, burning the bottom half of his own robe off in the process. Finbar hugged the pant-less wizard in hysteric relief. The wizard hugged him back, but only for a moment. With the entire city burning all around them, they were far from saved. There was precious little time left in which to escape.

Finbar hitched a ride out of the unrelenting inferno on the back of the wizard's horse. The pair sped through the shambles of the once great city, now the very picture of hell. Most of the main thoroughfares were blocked with collapsed buildings. Those that weren't blocked looked like swollen streams of fuming magma. Charred corpses littered the few accessible roads they did find. It took careful navigation on the part of the wizard to guide them from the center of the city to the outskirts. They rode through a narrow network of alleyways and winding streets, on those few remaining paths that had yet to be destroyed by the dragon. I say *yet*, because everything would eventually be destroyed. The dragon was still hard at work, with nothing to stop him. Finbar cowered in terror every time the monstrous shadow passed overhead.

They rode without rest until they reached the borders of the city. There they saw a seemingly endless trail of refugees leading off into the distant reaches of a hilly forest. They galloped along the trail until they reached a hilltop at the outskirts of the woods. Once there, safely hidden under the canopy of leaves, they finally stopped to rest.

Finbar rolled off the wizard's horse in exhaustion. He lay there in the soft, wavy grass, heart still bulging, too tired and traumatized to move. It was the saddest, happiest day of his life. He had gone from twice condemned, first by the chief inquisitor, then by the dragon, to having been twice saved, first from the burning stake, then from the burning city itself, and all in just a matter of hours. When it was all over, the world was over with it.

Finbar finally settled down and stood up. The wizard was gone, but there were other refugees everywhere. They stood all around him on the hilltop, all staring off in the same direction, all still as statues. Finbar looked in the same direction as everyone else at a view of the city which defied imagination—a view of utter ruin. Fantasmagoria looked like Pompeii after the eruption of Vesuvius. Sparks danced above the city like swarms of hellish fireflies. Ash and smoke painted the sky grey. The streets looked like flowing quagmires of molten gold. There wasn't a corner of the city untouched by the dragon, yet the serpent still circled about, spouting fire here and there, burning this or that for mere sport. There was nothing to be salvaged from the once great city. There was nothing to go back to.

Finbar watched and wondered if all inquisitions ended in the destruction of everything. It seemed like a proper ending. The inquisition had burned and burned until there was nothing left to burn. Now everyone was truly the same. Inquisitors met the same grim fate as heretics. None were discriminated by the dragon. Trolls, goblins, elves, fairies and dwarves were all the same in his eyes. Equality for all, finally. The Ministry of Equality's mission had ultimately been achieved, albeit by an unexpected, unforgiving means.

Finbar set forth into the wilderness with the remaining survivors. He was reunited with Ivan the editor-in-chief, Woodrow the wizard, and a handful of friends from the Tipsy Timepiece Tavern. All were mournful at the ruination of Fantasmagoria and the deaths of most of its citizens, yet many were relieved at the downfall of the inquisition and government. The religious reign of terror, widespread madness, and fear-based culture was finally over.

As Finbar hiked through the woods, he felt a newfound sense of freedom. In fact, he felt freer than he'd ever imagined possible. And it wasn't the dingy dungeon he felt free from, or even the troll tribunal. He felt free of the past. Everyone felt that same way—untethered from history. The past was truly dead. All that remained was the future. The refugees marched on, speaking hopefully of what lay ahead, and it seemed to Finbar everything would be alright. It seemed to him that out there in the wilderness, all the surviving creatures were as they were meant to be. They were themselves, and there was more harmony in that than could be forced with a thousand inquisitions.

A Sea Shanty

There was one refugee far, far from all the rest.

He didn't know he was refugee. He was as old as they come. A retired lighthouse keeper, he came outdoors only in the wind. You see, he had once loved a mermaid, and the wind reunited him with her by the magic of a secret sea spell cast long ago. The old man had left Fantasmagoria after the wind was canceled, in search of his mermaid. After enduring many hardships and adventures, he made it all the way back to his lighthouse at the end of the world.

Too old to climb the lighthouse, the old man sat on the shore waiting hopelessly for the winds to blow as they used to. To his surprise, they did. The winds started again as soon as Fantasmagoria was leveled by the dragon. The old man was lucky. It was that time of year when the winds blew toward the lighthouse shore, bringing forth all flavors of delectable fish from the ocean depths. A curiously strong wind blew that day, as if making up for lost time. There was a hint of something clammy in those squalls.

The old man sat there with his feet in the sand, fingers of zephyr coursing through his thin hair, submerged once again by the mermaid's enchantment. He closed his eyes and found himself on the sea floor. It was very dark. He looked hopelessly for his mermaid, but she was nowhere to be found. All he could see a few feet from him was a speck of light glowing faintly, so he swam toward it. As he drew closer, he saw it was shaped like a fairy. The thing was no bigger than a goldfish, but with the face and shape of a girl and little wings acting as fins on its back. The old man reached out to touch the creature. It smiled cleverly, before biting his finger. *Hard.*

The old man opened his eyes in surprise. Before

him, there in the water just off the shore, was a mermaid. *His* mermaid. She swam to him, giving him one of those briny mermaid kisses. And that kiss was no ordinary kiss. That kiss was a last kiss, and last kisses are more powerful than anything, with the possible exception of first kisses. That particular last kiss was so potent, the old man's spirit left his exhausted old man body, once and for all.

The mermaid lay the old man down in the sand, his eyes half-closed, a fishy smile on his face. She leaned over him and sang a sea shanty, the way she used to. And when the old man's ghost reached that legendary afterlife of seafarers called Fiddler's Green, where music plays to the end of time and dancers never tire, it was her voice that sang for him.

Many a mariner crowned a mermaid his own capstan queen,
Trolls, goblins, dwarves, elves, a man from Skibbereen,
Rising on the ocean waves before sinking to Fiddler's Green.

Some fell from the mizzen,
Others were lost at sea.
One was eaten by a kraken,
You were just old as can be.

Parading down around hell, the seaman can
be seen,
There they all look quite the same—slimy and
serene,
Hurrying their way to heaven, the mirth of
Fiddler's Green.

And so when sailors meet their maker in the
depths unseen,
She wears the scales of a fish and the face of
a siren queen,
Dancing to a song that never ends, the lay of
Fiddler's Green.

Steve Wiley, Author

Steve is a writer from Chicagoland, where he still lives with his wife and two kids. Publishers Weekly called his first novel, *The Fairytale Chicago of*

Francesca Finnegan, "Intelligent, enchanting, and playful." Wiley's second novel, *The Imagined Homecoming of Icarus Isakov*, was released in the spring of 2020. His short fiction has been published everywhere from Crannóg magazine in Galway, Ireland, to Papercuts magazine in Pakistan. Steve has an undergraduate degree in something he has forgotten from Illinois State University and a graduate degree in something equally forgotten from DePaul University. Steve once passionately kissed a bronze seahorse in the middle of Buckingham Fountain. Seriously, he did.

You can follow Steve's work at absurdistfiction.com.

Work Cited

Ancient Stoic Truth Missiles. Retrieved from: https://highexistence.com/47-ancient-stoic-truth-missiles/

Aurelius, Marcus. *Meditations*. United States: Dover Publications, 1997.

First Cavalry Division. "Fiddlers Green." *U.S. Army Cavalry Journal*, 1923.

Gay Vampire Joke. Retrieved from: https://www.reddit.com/r/Jokes/comments/ek8yhb

/what_do_you_call_a_gay_vampire/

Murray, Douglas. *The Madness of Crowds*. United States: Bloomsbury Continuum, 2019.

Padraic O'Liffey Joke. Retrieved from: https://upjoke.com/flaherty-jokes

Parker Jr., Ray. Ghostbusters. On Ghostbusters: Original Soundtrack Album. Arista, 1984

Cheap Trick. Dream Police. On Dream Police. Epic, 1979.

Stoicism. Retrieved from: https://en.wikipedia.org/wiki/Stoicism

Stoicism Antidote for Victimhood. Retrieved from: https://alexanderadamsart.wordpress.com/2018/09/28/stoicism-antidote-for-victimhood/

Wang Chung. Dance Hall Days. On Points on the Curve. Geffen, 1984.

What is Stoicism. Retrived fom: https://dailystoic.com/what-is-stoicism-a-definition-3-stoic-exercises-to-get-you-started/